**"To hell with your job,"
Carne snapped at her.**

"That means more to you than anything,
doesn't it? You're one of those females
who need to prove themselves in a
man's world! Who can't see there's
more to being a woman than competing
with a man."

"I wouldn't expect you to see it any other
way!" Lesley retorted hotly. "But those
chauvinist ideas are out of date. The
men I associate with judge a woman on
her ability, not her sex! Like any
civilized—"

"Oh, civilized!" He glared at her. "I'm
sick of hearing that word. Particularly
as every time you use it, you imply that
I'm not!"

"And are you?" she taunted recklessly.
"Would you call what you're doing to
me civilized?"

Other titles by

ANNE MATHER
IN HARLEQUIN PRESENTS

Other titles by

ANNE MATHER
IN HARLEQUIN ROMANCES

◆

ANNE MATHER

proud harvest

Harlequin Books

TORONTO · LONDON · NEW YORK · AMSTERDAM
SYDNEY · HAMBURG · PARIS

Harlequin Presents edition published November 1978
ISBN-0-373-70762-2

Original hardcover edition published in 1978
by Mills & Boon Limited

Printed in U.S.A.

CHAPTER ONE

'But he is Carne's son, Lesley,' Mrs Matthews exclaimed in the same tone of frustrated affection she often used to her grandson. 'Surely that means something to you.'

Lesley finished her coffee before replying, regarding her mother over the rim of the coffee cup with hazel eyes presently darkened to brown with impatience. The long curling lashes did nothing to disguise the indignation burning in their depths, and Mrs Matthews shifted rather uncomfortably under their penetrating gaze.

'What are you trying to say, Mother?' Lesley enquired at last, setting down the fragile cup in its equally fragile saucer. 'Has the idea of babysitting begun to pall?'

'To pall, no!' Mrs Matthews was offended now, wrapping the folds of her satin wrapper about her, putting a nervous hand up to touch the immaculately combed set of her hair. 'It's just that—well, as I say, he is Carne's son, and I see no reason why he shouldn't be allowed to spend at least part of the holiday with his father——'

'*You* see no reason!' Lesley's eyes sparkled angrily now. 'And what about me? Don't I have any say in the matter?'

'Oh, of course you do.' Mrs Matthews made a sound of exasperation with her tongue against her teeth. 'It was just a suggestion, that's all. I might have expected you would react emotionally instead of rationally. Lesley, people can be practical about these things, you know. Why, if everyone behaved as you do, the world would be in a very sorry state!'

'And isn't it?'

Mrs Matthews rose from the breakfast table with a sigh, and went to get herself one of the small cigars she favoured from the carved onyx box on the mantelpiece. Lighting it with the heavy silver lighter that squatted beside the cigar box, she drew on it deeply before turning to face her daughter again.

'I don't intend to get involved in reactionary discussion with you, Lesley,' she stated at last, holding her head stiffly. 'As I say, I thought you might see reason——'

'Reason!' Lesley bestowed another irritated glare in her mother's direction and then rose abruptly from the table. She was late. It was after nine already and she still had to get across town. She'd never make it, but with luck Lance wouldn't be in before ten as it was Monday morning, and there was nothing spoiling.

Brushing the crumbs from the skirt of her brown suede suit, she turned to face Mrs Matthews. 'Don't you know those things are bad for your health?' she exclaimed acidly, but her mother merely pulled a face.

'Why should I worry about my health?' she retorted. 'No one else does.'

Lesley, on her way to the door, halted uncertainly. 'Now what is that supposed to mean?' Her brows drew together in sudden concern. 'You're not—ill, are you?'

Mrs Matthews sniffed. 'Would you care if I was?'

'Oh, Mother!' Lesley glanced helplessly at her watch. 'I don't have time for discussion right now.' Talking about Jeremy had already taken up far too much time. 'Can't we leave this until later?'

'That's what I mean,' declared her mother peevishly. 'You never have time for anything—or anybody. Why, even your own son is a nuisance——'

'*Mother!*' Lesley's angry interjection cut her off in full spate. She reached for her handbag with hands which she found to her annoyance were trembling, and slung the strap over her shoulder. Then she looked at her mother again. 'I'll see you around five-thirty, right?'

Her voice was cool and although Mrs Matthews inclined her head in silent assent, she did not reply. Lesley hesitated only a moment longer and then wrenched open the door and left the room, closing it with a decided click behind her.

The lifts were all engaged, and she fretted impatiently until one chose to stop at the fourth floor. Downstairs, she barely answered the hall porter's greeting as he pulled open the door for her, and his eyes watched her doubtfully as she hastened down the shallow steps to the pavement. It wasn't like Mrs Radley to rush past him like that, and he hoped nothing had happened to that young son of hers. She had looked upset, and his brows drew together in a sympathetic frown. Always cheerful, that was Mrs Radley, always interested to hear about his wife and his family, never too busy to listen, not like some he could mention. That mother of hers, for example. Thought she was a cut above everybody else, she did. Well, what if her husband had been a brigadier? He was long dead now, and she was just plain Mrs Matthews. Her daughter, she was a different kettle of fish altogether. And that son of hers—regular little tearaway, he was. Pity her marriage hadn't worked out, but that was the way of it these days. Girls weren't content to stay at home and look after their families. They wanted a career, too. Equality. He grinned wryly. When were men going to be made equal? that's what he wanted to know.

Meanwhile, Lesley was reversing her Mini out of the underground parking area that adjoined the block of flats, totally unaware of having aroused such strong feelings. Her own feelings occupied her thoughts to the exclusion of everything else, and in consequence she almost ran into the back of a grey Jaguar parked opposite. Jamming on her brakes, she took several calming breaths before making a second attempt to turn, and her delay was heralded by several irate horns from other commuters baulked by her incompetence.

'All right, all right,' she groaned frustratedly to herself, as a cream Cortina nudged closer, and most ungentlemanly signs were made to her to move on. 'What a start to the week!' she muttered, and glancing in the rear-view mirror bestowed a smile of annoying tolerance on the driver of the vehicle behind.

But as she cleared the garage and joined the press of motorists streaming towards the underpass, her brief moment of stimulation passed and she found herself worrying over the things her mother had said. Perhaps she had been hasty. Perhaps she did expect too much of her mother. But without her assistance, what could she do? She couldn't afford a full-time nanny, even for holidays. The school fees alone were disastrous, and without Carne's contribution, Jeremy would have to have gone to a day school, which would have caused more problems. Of course, that was what Carne would have preferred, but she refused to admit that his feelings had played any part in her determination to send her son to boarding school.

Anyway, Jeremy was there now, and had been for almost a year. He hadn't seemed to take any harm from it. He was certainly a self-possessed little boy, but weren't all children nowadays? In any case, there had been no alternative, so that particular aspect of the matter was not worth considering. Holidays were something else again.

Lesley chewed unhappily at her lower lip. What would

she do if her mother refused to look after Jeremy? Who could she turn to? They had no other relatives, not on their side of the family anyway. And she could hardly ask one of Carne's sisters to have him while refusing his own father the opportunity. She sighed. She would not let him go to Carne, though. She *couldn't*! Ploughing through cow-pats all day long, mucking out stables, rolling about in the hay! His clothes would be ruined in no time, and she had no money to buy him new ones. No—somehow she had to make her mother see that proposition for what it was. Besides—a small expletive escaped her as a taxi swerved across her path and turned his thumb up at her—it was extremely doubtful that Carne would even consider it after not seeing his son for almost three years.

The Mini swept down the underpass and joined the jam at the other side. But it was gradually moving and she dropped down into bottom gear and allowed the wheels to maintain a steady roll forward. In spite of her preoccupation with her own problems, she became aware of someone watching her. Turning her head, she encountered the admiring stare of a young man in an exotic sports car cruising beside her in the next lane. Having attracted her attention, he kissed his fingers to his lips in an extravagant gesture, and she guessed he wasn't English. But it was good to know that in spite of her harassed feelings she could still attract the admiration of a handsome man, and her fingers went automatically to touch the honey-gold strands of hair that lay over her shoulder. Straight hair it was, but expertly cut to accentuate the oval shape of her face and tilt gently beneath the curve of her jawline. Her lips parted in a faint smile, and then there was a sickening crunch right ahead of her and she realised she had run into the back of the car in front. At the same moment the second stream of traffic surged ahead and her handsome admirer left her to face the purpling countenance of the middle-aged owner with the dented fender.

'Women drivers!' he grumbled, as she got out to face him. 'Well? I'm not paying for this.'

Lesley assured him that it was all her fault and he was somewhat mollified. She gave him her address, and the address of her insurance company, and then examined the damage to her own car. One of her headlights was broken, and her own fender dented, and as the man drove away she reflected that as usual she had come off worst. In addition to which her insurance premium was bound to be increased next time, and she got back behind the wheel wondering whether it wouldn't be simpler just to use a cab. But one could never get a cab at this hour of the morning, and besides, when Jeremy was on holiday she liked it for getting about . . .

Jeremy.

Depression swamped her once again. Whoever would have thought that one small boy could cause so much heartache? But she loved him desperately, and she was determined to keep him. Somehow she would make arrangements for the holidays, even if it meant bringing him to the office with her. That wouldn't go down too well, of course, and it would be hard on Jeremy having to keep quiet for hours on end. But she was confident that Lance would not sack her out of hand, she was too valuable to him, and if it was a matter of one or the other, she was sure he would not object. Eight weeks was not so long, and three of those she would be on holiday herself. She found her fingers crossing on the steering wheel. It might never come to that. Her mother would not *refuse* to have him. Just because at Easter he had broken her Chinese vase . . . and poured salt into the sugar bowl . . .

and played Red Indians with her ostrich feathers . . . and smuggled that disgusting little mongrel into the flat and hidden him under his bed . . .

Lesley hunched her shoulders. Perhaps he was too high-spirited for a woman of sixty to handle. Particularly a woman who had already worn herself out looking after her own child, or so she said. Lesley sighed. Had she been such a trial? She had quite fond memories of her youth. Of course, her father had been alive in those days and he and she seemed so much alike. Perhaps it was the later years, after her father was dead, when she had been at university. Her mother had hated all the sit-ins and demonstrations she had joined. Mrs Matthews' politics were so arbitrarily conservative and she had been appalled by the left-wing young Socialists Lesley had brought to the house. She had not realised that it was all a phase. That an active mind demanded activity, of whatever persuasion. But in one respect her anxieties had been realised. Lesley had remained staunchly independent in her attitude towards men and Mrs Matthews had been convinced she would never get married. It would have been better if she hadn't, Lesley thought now, not without some bitterness. Then Jeremy would never have been born, never have become the problem he was today. And yet . . . She drew the Mini to a jerky halt at the barrier marking the precincts of W.L.T.V. and forced a smile for the security officer as he raised the barrier for her. If she was honest with herself she would admit that she did not entirely regret those years with Carne. They had been an experience she was not likely to forget. And should she ever be tempted to do so, Jeremy—her darling Jeremy—was there to remind her.

She had still not got over the thrill of seeing her name on her parking lot. *Mrs Lesley Radley*, it read, right alongside

Lance Petrie, Controller of Programmes. Her official designation was Personal Private Secretary, but she was more than that. She was his right hand, his assistant, the person everyone came to who wanted an audience with the big man. She was fortunate, she knew that. If she hadn't worked at W.L.T.V. years ago she would never have stood a chance of getting where she was today after only two years. But Lance remembered her, and forgave her for walking out on him.

As she crossed the concrete apron of the car park to the swing glass doors of the executive building, she remembered how aggressive she had been when she first came here eight years ago—twenty years of age, straight out of university with a degree in both arts and languages, confident that she could change the face of civilisation. Lance had been the producer of a current affairs programme in those days, and she had applied for a job as his assistant. When he had asked her what she knew about news and broadcasting she had arrogantly maintained that she had what was lacking in television today—a fresh eye, an unbiased view, an original approach. He had been amused by her ignorance, she realised now, flattered by her determination to work for him, and willing to give youth a chance to prove itself. Within six months, he had changed her whole outlook on life, showing her the cracks in both the socialist and capitalist systems, making her aware that government in any form was ultimately a victim of its own prejudices. She had learned with him and from him, until that fateful day they drove north to Yorkshire to interview a young farmer with radical views on Britain's entry into the European Common Market . . .

The wide, chequerboard tiling of the hall reflected the watery rays of a sun just struggling to clear the clouds that lingered after last night's rainstorm. Lesley smiled at the receptionist, asked Albert, the commissionaire, how his arthritis was faring in this damp weather, and took the lift up to the penthouse floor.

Lance had done just as well as she, she thought now, entering the panelled outer office where she had her desk. From current affairs producer to Controller of Programmes in seven years was not bad going. Still he deserved it, she decided generously, taking off her jacket and hanging it on the stand. He was well informed and well liked, and no one else at W.L.T.V. would have taken her back after abandoning her career like any lovesick schoolgirl.

Her boss was not in, as she had hoped, and she had sorted through the pile of mail on her desk and laid aside those requiring his personal attention before he put in an appearance. Lance Petrie was a big man, both W.L.T.V.-wise and physically. Easily six feet in height, he rarely took any exercise, and in consequence years of liquid lunches and business dinners had put on several inches of girth. He had bristling ginger eyebrows and a voice that could strike fear into the strongest constitution, but Lesley had long learned that his bark was worse than his bite. He never did anyone a bad turn, unless they had done him one first, and his friends at W.L.T.V. numbered larger than his enemies, which was quite something for a man in his position.

Now he ambled into Lesley's office with deceptive deliberation, and after answering her proffered 'Good morning' he looked over his shoulder at the letters she was studying.

'Anything interesting?' he enquired, and she cast a swift look up at him before replying: 'Only this invitation to speak at the Guild Luncheon. They must have enjoyed your speech last year to ask you to make a repeat performance.'

'Hmm.' Lance sounded doubtful. He leant over and flicked the invitation aside. 'Car going okay?'

His change of subject was so abrupt that the sound Lesley was about to make became strangled in her throat. When she could speak, she said faintly: 'My car?'

'Whose else?' He straightened. 'Well? Is it?'

Lesley sighed. 'By that I gather you know it's not,' she exclaimed, and the heavy brow furrowed.

'No.' He shook his head. 'It was an innocent question. I just wondered why you were late this morning as well as Friday.'

'Oh!' Lesley's cheeks went pink. 'You were in earlier.'

'I was here at nine-thirty, yes,' Lance agreed, thrusting his big hands into the pockets of his jacket and consequently pulling it all out of shape. 'So what's happened with the Mini? Don't I pay you enough to keep it in working order?'

Lesley moved her shoulders apologetically. 'I had a bump,' she confessed. 'I ran into the back of one of those foreign cars. I don't know what it was, but I bent the fender.'

'And that's why you were late?'

Lesley hesitated. 'Well—no.' She looked up at him honestly. 'It's Jeremy, actually.'

'Jeremy?' Lance looked concerned. 'He's not ill, is he?'

'Oh, no. No.' Lesley made a rueful sound. 'If only it were that easy! No, he's due home for the holidays in ten days' time, and—my mother has decided it's too much for her to have him around the flat all day.'

'I see,' Lance nodded. Like Lesley, he too had been married, but perhaps fortunately his wife had been unable to have children and when they split up, no one had been hurt but themselves. 'I guess he is a bit of a handful for a woman of her age.'

Lesley fiddled with the papers on her desk. 'Yes.'

'And there's no one else who could care for him while you're working?'

She shook her head. 'No.'

'What about his father——'

'Oh, please . . .' Lesley felt she couldn't go through all that again. 'Carne doesn't want him. Besides, it wouldn't be fair to ask him. Not after all this time.'

'Why not? Jeremy's his son, too.'

'I know, but—well, Jeremy would be unhappy.'

'Why should he be? With animals to care for and all those acres to run free across! My God, it's any boy's dream, Lesley. He'd soon adapt, you'd see.'

'No.'

'What do you mean—no?' Lance stared at her consideringly for several unnerving seconds, then he uttered an astonished laugh. 'Dammit, you're scared!' he exclaimed. 'You don't want to ask Radley because you're afraid the boy will enjoy himself.'

'Oh, don't talk such nonsense!' exclaimed Lesley, forgetting for the moment to whom she was speaking. Then: 'I'm sorry, but—please, Lance, this is my affair. Let me handle it my way.'

Lance gave a disgruntled snort. 'You're getting possessive, do you know that?' he told her provokingly. 'If you're not careful, you'll turn into one of those jealous old women who cling to their sons like leeches, and try to pretend they don't need a husband!'

Lesley gasped. 'What a rotten thing to suggest!'

'But apt, wouldn't you say?' he countered, rocking backwards and forwards on his heels and toes.

'I'm twenty-eight, Lance. Not exactly in my dotage yet, you know.'

'And Jeremy's seven—I know. But in thirty years' time, you mark my words . . .'

Nodding annoyingly to himself, he went into his office and closed the door, and Lesley applied herself with unnecessary aggression to her typing. But her fingers kept hitting the wrong keys, and she was glad when Elizabeth came round with the tea-trolley and she could give herself a break before continuing.

There was a production meeting at eleven, and as Lance's secretary she was expected to take notes, so that filled the rest of the morning in. Then, in the afternoon, Lance gave her some dictation, and finished by apologising for criticising her that morning.

'It's all right,' insisted Lesley stiffly, but Lance was determined to make amends.

'It's not all right,' he argued. 'I don't have any children, so how the hell can I pass judgment on anyone who has. Look, if it's any help, you could bring him into the office a couple of days every week. So long as he sat quietly while you were working—he could bring books and crayoning pencils, couldn't he? I guess you're not working all the time, and maybe it would be possible for you to take an extra day off here and there . . .'

'Oh, Lance!' His unexpected understanding was disarming. 'I don't know what to say.'

'Don't say anything,' he advised gruffly. 'I'll probably regret it bitterly. Now, will you get Manders on the phone? I want to know why *The Mike Harris Show* has dropped out of the top ten ratings.'

For once there were no last-minute problems to attend to and when Lance came into her office at four o'clock it was to tell her that she could go and see about getting her car fixed, if she liked.

'Go to Henleys and mention my name,' he said. 'Tell them you need it urgently. And I'm not joking. I expect you to be at your desk on time in the morning, car or no car.'

'Yes, Mr Petrie.' Lesley hid her smile, but for all that, she knew he meant it. Punctuality was one thing he demanded.

Outside, the pavements were bathed in bright sunshine. Carrying her jacket, she got into the Mini and drove to the garage Lance had suggested. It wasn't far from the studios, and the owner knew her employer very well. They were old drinking cronies, and a calculated examination of her car solicited the information that he could have it ready for the following afternoon.

'Will it be very expensive?' asked Lesley anxiously, recalling her mounting insurance premium, but the man shook his head.

'Tell your boss I'll make up the difference on that old banger of his next time he brings it in for a service,' he retorted with a grin, but Lesley doubted Lance would appreciate such humour when it was directed towards the vintage Rolls-Royce he had rescued from the scrap heap. Still, she returned the man's smile and thanked him for his help and then hurried away to Baker Street station to take the underground to Russell Square.

It was still barely five o'clock when she turned into St Anne's Gate and saw the soaring block of apartments where her mother had chosen to move six years ago. Once her daughter was comfortably married, Mrs Matthews had seen no reason to keep on the small house in Hampstead, or at least that was her story. Lesley knew that she had been finding it hard to make ends meet, and the sum the sale of the house had raised had given her a nice little nest-egg.

The pension she received was not large, but that together with the interest from her capital had ensured she would not starve. What she had not bargained for was that Lesley might return home only two years after she had moved into the flat bringing with her a lively two-year-old who had been used to the kind of freedom a city flat could not provide.

Lesley sighed. Perhaps she should have found her own place, maintained the independence she had guarded so jealously. But when she left Carne she had needed some place to hide, and her mother had seemed the most natural person to turn to. And indeed, Mrs Matthews had been very tolerant, she conceded, taking Jeremy to and from his nursery school, babysitting when Lesley had had to work late or at weekends. But they were all growing older, and as her mother had less patience, Jeremy demanded more.

A dust-smeared Citroën station wagon was parked out front of the apartments and Lesley's eyes flickered over it speculatively. Someone cared about their car even less than she did, she thought with satisfaction, noticing the clutter of maps and old cartons in the back, the magazines strewn haphazardly across the rear seat. Farming magazines they were, she saw in passing. She mounted the steps to the swing doors and smiled as the hall porter came to open the door for her.

'How are you, Mr Peel?' she asked, with genuine interest, and his monologue concerning their Sandra's grumbling appendix carried her into the lift.

But as the metal casing hummed easily up to the fourth floor, her thoughts returned irresistibly to the station wagon outside. It was such a coincidence that it should be there today when every free moment seemed to have been filled with thoughts of Carne, and Jeremy, and the life she had run away from. She shifted her weight from one foot to the other, refusing to admit that Lance's accusation had scraped a nerve. She wasn't afraid of Jeremy's reactions to his father. Good heavens, he scarcely remembered him after all this time. They would have nothing in common—just as she and Carne had had nothing in common . . .

The lift whispered to a halt and the doors slid open. Pushing her weight away from the wall of the lift, she stepped out into the corridor, smelling the familiar, if not particularly agreeable, smell of pine disinfectant. The flat she shared with her mother was several yards down and she sauntered towards it slowly, her brows drawn together in a frown. Why should she be letting Lance's words disturb her like this? After all, Carne had stopped seeing his son, not the other way about. Why should she blame herself if he chose to ignore their existence, and most particularly, why should she feel any guilt because Jeremy was growing up knowing nothing of the land that was his heritage? His heritage was hers, a heritage of city things and city people. Everyone said that this was where it was all happening. People converged on London from all over the world. Jeremy might never know how to plough a field or wean a foal, but then he probably wouldn't want to.

She found her key and inserted it in the lock and the door opened silently into the tiny entrance hall of the flat. The hall was made tinier by her mother's insistence on keeping an old chest, inlaid with ivory, which Lesley's father had brought back from India, but it reduced the floor space to a minimum. Last holidays, Jeremy had hidden inside it and terrified them all by falling asleep and almost suffocating himself.

Lesley was closing the door again when the sound of voices coming from the living room attracted her attention. It was so unusual for her mother to have callers. She seldom

associated with her neighbours, and Lesley usually knew
when one or other of her friends from Hampstead days was
expected to call. Besides, Lesley hesitated, it sounded like a
man's voice . . .

Her mouth went dry, and she deliberately closed the door
so that they should not hear her. A cascade of staggering
thoughts was tumbling through her head—the conversation
with her mother that morning, the dusty station wagon outside, with the farming magazines spread over the seat, and
now a man's voice.

It was Carne. She was sure of it. She would know his low
husky drawl anywhere. Hadn't she always admired his voice,
its throbbing timbre which had had the power to send
shivers of excitement up her spine. But no longer, she reminded herself severely. She was no eager student any
longer, she was a grown woman, mature and she hoped,
sophisticated. So what was he doing here? Had her mother
sent for him? Of course, she was home earlier than they
could have expected. It was usually nearing six by the time
she had negotiated the rush hour traffic.

She turned quickly, and as she did so she saw her reflection in the convex mirror hanging above the Indian chest.
Wide, anxious eyes stared back at her, lips parted apprehensively. Impatience brought a frown to her forehead. Why
did she look so anxious? Why should she be apprehensive?
She had nothing to fear. So why did she suddenly feel like
letting herself out of the flat again as quietly as she had
come in?

Biting her lips to give them a little colour, she ran a
smoothing hand over the heavy curtain of her hair, and
turned to the door. She put out her hand, hesitated, and
withdrew it again. Unwillingly, she could hear their voices
now, and shamelessly she was listening.

'Lesley simply doesn't know,' she heard her mother saying, a sigh of resignation in her voice. 'I couldn't bring myself to tell her.'

'Then you must.' Carne was always so unfailingly practical, thought Lesley maliciously. 'She's not a child. She would understand.'

'I don't believe she would.' Mrs Matthews paused, and Lesley grew impatient for her to continue. What wouldn't she understand? And how could her mother discuss it with Carne and not with her?

'Do you want me to tell her?'

Carne was speaking again, and Lesley could stand it no longer. Whatever was going on, she was involved and therefore she had the right to know about it. With trembling fingers, her hand closed round the handle, and she propelled the door inward.

CHAPTER TWO

CARNE was standing on the rug in front of the marble fireplace. The fire was seldom lit, there being a perfectly adequate heating system supplied to the flats from a central generator, and besides, no one needed a fire in summer. In consequence, the grate was screened and Carne's long, powerful legs were outlined against a ridiculously fragile tracery of Chinese fans embroidered on to a turquoise background. Lesley's mother collected Eastern things, and the room was a conglomeration of Japanese jade and Indian ivory, and hand-painted Chinese silk. Their oriental delicacy made Carne's presence more of an intrusion somehow, and his height and lean, but muscular, body seemed to fill the space with disruptive virility. Standing there in close-fitting jeans and a collarless body shirt, he was an affront to the ordered tenor of the room, and most particularly an affront to Lesley's carefully controlled existence.

She barely glanced at him, yet in those few seconds she registered everything about him. He hadn't changed, she thought bitterly. He was still as imperturbably arrogant as ever, caring little for people or places, showing a fine contempt for the things she had always held most dear. In spite of a degree in biochemistry, when his father died Carne had been quite prepared to give up a promising scientific career to take over the farm that had been in their family for generations, but Lesley, when she learned this, had been horrified. It had been one of the many arguments she had had with Carne's mother, yet hardly a conclusive factor in her final decision to leave him. She knew deep inside her that there had been much more to it than that, an accumulation of so many things that clutching at his lack of ambition was like clutching at a straw in the wind. They had been incompatible, she decided, choosing the most hackneyed word to describe the breakdown of their relationship.

Now, looking at her mother, who had risen rather nervously from her chair, she exclaimed: 'Exactly what must I be told, Mother? What is it that I wouldn't understand?'

By ignoring Carne, she hoped she was making plain her resentment at finding him here, but it was he who spoke as her mother struggled to find words.

'Listening at keyholes again, Lesley?' he taunted, and she could not argue with that.

'You're home early, dear.'

Her mother had clearly chosen to avoid a direct answer, but Lesley refused to be put off by Carne's attempt to disarm her.

'Why is Carne here?' she demanded, returning to the attack, and she sensed rather than saw the look Mrs Matthews exchanged with her husband. There was a pregnant pause, then he spoke again.

'Your mother has angina,' he told her flatly, despite her mother's cry of protest. 'A heart condition that's not improved by the company of a boisterous small boy!'

Lesley's legs felt suddenly weak, and she sought the back of her mother's chair for support. 'Angina?' she echoed stupidly. Then: 'But why wasn't I told?'

'I imagine because your mother hoped you would notice she wasn't well,' Carne remarked cuttingly. 'It's one thing to shout about independence, and quite another to expect someone else to help you to accomplish it!'

Lesley stared at him indignantly, hating him for his calm

pragmatism. His returning stare had all the emotion of a hawk poised above its prey, and she guessed he felt no sympathy for her feelings of outrage and betrayal. How could her mother have confided in him? In the one man who in all Lesley's life had been capable of making her feel mean and selfish, and spoiled out of all measure.

'Why have you come here?' she demanded again now, and this time her mother chose to answer.

'I asked him to,' she spoke fretfully. 'Oh, Lesley, don't be angry. I had to confide in someone.'

It was incredibly difficult for Lesley not to show how upset she really was. 'Why not me?' she exclaimed, with feeling. 'Why not me?'

'I believe your mother thought that if she could persuade you to let Jeremy spend his holidays at Raventhorpe, it wouldn't be necessary to worry you,' put in Carne dryly. 'But I gather that hasn't met with any success.'

Lesley refused to answer that. Instead, she concentrated her attention on her mother. 'Look,' she said carefully, 'I've —I've managed to make some—arrangements for the holidays——'

'What sort of arrangements?'

It was Carne who asked the question, pushing back the dark chestnut hair from his forehead, unwillingly drawing her attention to the fact that when he lifted his arm, his shirt separated from his pants and exposed a welt of brown midriff. Carne's skin had always been brown, but as he often worked in the open air with only a pair of cotton pants to protect his lower limbs, his chest and shoulders and the width of his back were bronzed and supple. In spite of all the bitterness that had gone before, she could still remember the feel of that smooth skin beneath her fingers and her nails digging into the strong muscles when they made love . . .

Dragging her eyes away from him, she forced herself to look only at her mother. 'I—I spoke to Lance today,' she began, and felt a certain squalid satisfaction as she sensed Carne's stiffening. 'He—he's quite willing for me to take Jeremy to the office with me. He can read or use his cray——'

'No.'

Carne's rejection was low, but succinct, and Lesley was forced to acknowledge it. 'I don't think it's anything to do with you.'

'Which shows how wrong you can be,' he retorted smoothly.

'Oh, please . . .' Mrs Matthews sought her chair again. 'I never intended this to degenerate into an argument. I know how you feel about Jeremy, Lesley, never doubt that. But Carne was the right person to turn to, can't you see? He is the boy's father!'

Lesley's eyes sparkled dangerously in Carne's direction for a moment, before she said: 'That's meant a lot to him in recent years, hasn't it. Or has he been seeing Jeremy behind my back, too?'

'Lesley!' Carne's voice was grim, and briefly she felt ashamed.

'I'm sorry,' she said stiffly, addressing her mother. 'But you know as well as I do how often Carne has troubled to see Jeremy since I left Ravensdale——'

'You little bitch!' In a stride, Carne had covered the distance between them and was gripping her upper arms with fingers that dug cruelly into her flesh. 'You little bitch!' he repeated, less emotively, his gaze raking her shakily resentful features. 'You know as well as I do why I stopped seeing him. You'd confused him enough as it was. A father who appeared at weekends and holidays is no father at all to a toddler barely out of his nappies, and you know it.'

'That—that's your excuse, is it?' she got out jerkily, and his brown eyes darkened to appear almost black, filling the area around the dilated pupils with ominous obscurity.

'Yes, that's my excuse,' he agreed savagely. 'How do you salve your conscience, I wonder?'

Lesley tore herself away from him, rubbing her bruised arms with fingers that trembled. 'You always were a bully, weren't you, Carne?' she countered, but it was a defensive reaction, born of the desire to escape the physical awareness she had always had of him, an awareness heightened by the heated scent of his body and the raw sensuality of the man himself. It was an unconscious trait, but it was there, and she knew she was not the only woman to be aware of it.

Mrs Matthews was looking distinctly distressed now, and ignoring Lesley Carne turned to her. 'Do you want me to go?' he asked gently, but Lesley's muffled 'Yes' was overridden by her mother's hurried denial.

'Lesley had to know sooner or later,' she said, and pointed to the cigar box on the mantelpiece. 'Please—could I have one of those? I really need it.'

Lesley stood by feeling childishly sulky and admonished as Carne lit her mother's cheroot, but she couldn't deny the fluttery feelings in the pit of her stomach. She wondered what would have happened if she hadn't run the Mini into the back of the other car that morning, if she hadn't got out of work early and come home and surprised them. When would her mother have mentioned Carne's visit? When would she have revealed that her heart could not stand the demands put upon it by a child of Jeremy's age and temperament? When would she have disclosed that she was actually negotiating arrangements without even consulting her daughter!

Panic gave way to angry indignation once more. It was

as if she, Jeremy's mother, had no say in the matter. And Carne was obviously a willing accessory. And why not? It was, no doubt, exactly what he wanted. Once he and his mother got Jeremy to Ravensdale they would have eight weeks to work on him, eight weeks to twist everything Lesley had ever told him, eight weeks to turn him against the woman who had borne him. Self-pity swamped her. Carne's mother had always hated her, had always resented the fleeting hold she had had over her precious son. Jeremy was that son all over again, the grandson she had always wanted to be there to take over Raventhorpe when his father retired. The long tradition of the Radleys was weighted against her. What possible defence did she have against that?

Carne straightened from lighting her mother's cheroot and regarded her coldly. 'I suggest this matter needs further consideration,' he remarked, toying with the heavy lighter. 'I've arranged to stay in town overnight. I suggest we meet for dinner, like the civilised people we are supposed to be, and discuss what's to be done.'

Lesley stiffened her spine. 'So far as I'm concerned, there's nothing to discuss,' she retorted icily, but his gaze never faltered.

'I'm staying at the President,' he went on, mentioning the name of a comfortable three-star hotel in Russell Square. He glanced down at his casual attire. 'I need a drink and a shower, but I'll be back here to pick you up in—say, an hour and a half?'

Lesley licked her dry lips. 'You can't force me to go out with you, Carne.'

'For God's sake!' He swore angrily. 'I should have thought you'd have got over that childish temper of yours by now!'

'Why should I? You haven't.'

'Lesley . . .'

Mrs Matthews' fretful protest silenced any cutting retort Carne might have been about to make. Instead, controlling his anger with admirable skill, he said: 'I'll give you two hours, Lesley. That should be long enough for your mother to convince you that you can't go on running away from life's unpleasantnesses.'

'Like you, you mean?' she taunted, and then turned away, despising herself for behaving like a shrew. But it had been quite a day, and it wasn't over yet.

She heard Carne bidding her mother goodbye, and half turned as he let himself out of the apartment. His brooding gaze swept over her and found her lacking, and she concentrated her attention on her clenched fists as he closed the door behind him.

The room was strangely empty after he had gone, but her mother was there and her eyes were full of reproach.

'How could you, Lesley?' she exclaimed, pressing out the half smoked cheroot with unsteady fingers. 'Making a scene like that! I never thought you could be so—so vindictive!'

'Vindictive?' The word brought a sound of protest from Lesley's lips. 'Me? Vindictive?'

'Well, what would you call it?' Mrs Matthews demanded. '*I* asked Carne to come here, and this is my home, after all. How could you speak to a guest of mine in such a fashion?'

'A guest of yours?' Lesley stared at her ludicrously. 'Mother, Carne is my husband? Separated, it's true, but husband, nevertheless! You can't accuse me of being rude to my own husband!'

'I can, and what's more, I do,' declared her mother, with a sniff. 'I think Carne showed remarkable restraint in the face of outright provocation. Jeremy is his son as well as yours, Lesley, whether you like it or not. And any court in the land would grant him custodial rights if he chose to make a case of it.'

Lesley trembled. She couldn't help it. It sounded so cold-blooded somehow, and her mother had put her finger on the one thing she had always fought against considering.

'Carne—Carne doesn't need Jeremy,' she said now. 'I do.'

'Try convincing a magistrate of that.'

'Mother!' Lesley stared with anguished eyes. 'Mother, what are you trying to do? To make me give Jeremy up?'

Mrs Matthews shrugged. 'I'm just pointing out that Carne has been very patient, but I shouldn't push him any further if I were you.'

Lesley pressed her lips together for a moment. 'You mean —I should have dinner with him?'

'I mean that if Carne is willing to give the boy a home for the holidays, you should be glad to let him go.'

'But, Mother, the only time I see Jeremy is in the holidays!'

'That's nothing to do with me.' Mrs Matthews rose painfully to her feet. Her lumbago was troubling her today and so far as she was concerned, the discussion was over. 'I'm going to my room——'

'Wait!' Lesley took an automatic step forward. 'You—you still haven't told me about—about the angina.'

'There's nothing to tell.'

'But what did Dr Forrest say?'

'He said I should rest more. That I shouldn't get excited,' she added, with a returning look of reproof.

'Oh, Mother!' Lesley linked and unlinked her fingers. 'If you'd only told me . . .'

'What, and have you speak to me as you spoke to Carne!'

'That's not fair . . .'

Her mother made a dismissing gesture. 'I'm going to lie down. Don't bother about making me a meal. I'll get something later, if I'm hungry.'

Lesley watched her mother's progress across the room with troubled eyes. Not least among the many things that troubled her was the realisation that her mother could hide a thing like that from her—and for how long? That was another of the questions that still needed answering. With a despairing sigh, she sank down on to a low couch and pushed back the heavy weight of her hair with both hands. Was she really so unfeeling? Was she so wrapped up in her own affairs that she had no time for anyone else? She had never thought so, but now . . . It seemed incredible that that morning she had had no notion of what plans her mother had been nurturing, or indeed that even as she lunched in the staff canteen at W.L.T.V. Carne was at that moment driving down the M.1. from Yorkshire, intent on keeping an appointment which must have been made days ago. It hurt to think her mother could deceive her, and while she didn't seriously believe there had been other meetings, nevertheless a little of her trust had been undermined.

Leaving the cluttered paraphernalia of the living room, Lesley went into her bedroom, the room she shared with Jeremy when he was home. She supposed that situation would not be approved by a court of law, but as the flat only had two bedrooms, there was no other alternative. Short of sharing her mother's bedroom, of course, but naturally Mrs Matthews wanted a room to herself. If Lesley had thought of what might happen in the future, as Jeremy got too old to share her room, it was along the lines of them perhaps acquiring a larger apartment, but she had never really considered what she would do if her mother should object. Carne was right, in one way. Her independence did depend on her mother to a large extent at the moment, but once Jeremy was old enough to be left alone, she supposed there was no reason why they shouldn't get a flat of their own. But all these things had been hazy, nebulous, distant possibilities that would work themselves out in the natural order of things. Now all that had been changed, and suddenly she was faced with the practicalities of the present, and with the disturbing realisation that her mother had put all their futures into Carne's hands.

The bathroom was vacant and she turned on the taps to silence the frenzied screaming of her nerves. Sprinkling essence liberally into the bath water, she watched the deep green liquid melt and dissolve, to rise again as balls of foam that made a fluffy white carpet over the surface. What could she say to Carne to make him see that by reappearing in Jeremy's life now, he could only confuse the boy again? *Confuse?* Her lips twisted. She was confused. Carne already knew that. By springing her mother's illness upon her, he had successfully diluted her arguments, just as the bath water had diluted the essence.

It was a marvellous relief to sink down into the heated suds, and allow the softened water to probe every pore of her tense body. She needed to relax, to think coherently. She needed to restore every shred of composure before encountering her husband again.

It didn't help to realise that seeing him again had upset her more than she had expected. In the early days after their break-up she had seen him on several occasions, but always in the company of her mother and Jeremy, and in the aftermath of that final devastating row which had ended with her bundling Jeremy into her car and leaving, a defensive numbness had coated the more vulnerable areas of her emotions.

Maybe if she had had warning of the meeting, if she had

had time to gather herself, so to speak, so that when she faced him she had behaved with coolness and sophistication, and not given in to those entirely schoolgirlish taunts and provocations. Maybe then she would not be feeling so raw now, so exposed to all the pain and misery that had both preceded and followed her separation from Carne.

She lay in the bath too long and had to hurry with her dressing. Somehow she had accepted that she had to have dinner with him, if only to prevent her mother any more distress. That she had brought the distress on herself meant less than Lesley's guilty neglect of her mother's health, and after satisfying herself that she looked neither too young nor too sophisticated, she went into Mrs Matthews' bedroom.

Her mother was lying on the bed reading a magazine, and judging from her appearance, she seemed to have recovered from her earlier upset. Lesley hesitated in the doorway, not quite knowing what to say, and then she casually flicked the skirt of her flared jersey dress.

'Does this look all right?'

Mrs Matthews regarded her critically for a moment, over the top of the magazine. 'Shouldn't you wear a long gown?' she enquired, and Lesley expelled her breath on a long sigh.

'I don't think so,' she replied. 'After all, I don't know where we're going, do I?'

'I thought most young people wore long clothes these days,' averred her mother rather peevishly, and Lesley wondered if she was being deliberately obstructive.

'How are you feeling now?' she asked, changing the subject, but Mrs Matthews was still looking at her dress.

'I suppose it is pretty material,' she decided grudgingly. 'You always did suit blue and gold. But don't you think those sandals are too high? You may have to walk. Carne will probably leave his car at the hotel.'

Lesley examined the slender heels of the leather strapped sandals on her narrow feet. 'I thought they looked rather nice,' she murmured doubtfully, then, as the doorbell rang: 'Are you sure you're all right?'

'Don't start worrying about me now, Lesley,' her mother retorted shortly. 'You never have cared about anyone but yourself.'

The accusation was so hurtful that for a moment Lesley could only stare at her. Then the doorbell rang again, more peremptorily this time, and with a helpless shake of her head, she went to answer it.

But at least her mother's barb had one effect. It stiffened Lesley's failing resolve and the feeling of injustice that filled her gave her confidence to face whatever was to come.

Carne was leaning against the wall beside the door when she opened it, but he straightened at her appearance and she thought with a pang how like old times this was. Their attraction had been immediate and mutual, and every spare moment he had had, or could make, Carne had driven the two hundred or so miles to see her.

But that was all in the past. The Carne Radley who accepted her stiff invitation to step into the flat this evening was older and infinitely more mature, his dark brown mohair lounge suit as immaculate as his jeans had been casual earlier. A special occasion, then, she thought, with bitter humour. Carne didn't put on his best clothes for everybody. His detached gaze barely registered her appearance and she wondered if she'd not bothered to change whether he would have noticed.

Mrs Matthews appeared as Lesley went to collect a lacy scarf to put about her shoulders. She greeted Carne warmly, and Lesley wondered if she had any real feelings for Jeremy at all. Didn't her mother realise that by forcing her hand, she might create a situation none of them could control?

Jeremy had a mind of his own, but he was too young to be forced to choose. Carne had bowed out of his obligations. Why wouldn't her mother accept that?

When she came back, Carne was handing her mother a glass of the sherry she kept for special visitors, but Lesley noticed he wasn't drinking himself. Mrs Matthews sipped the glowing brown liquid delicately and asked whether all the rain they had been having had caused any problems. Carne explained that the ground had been very dry from the previous year and the absence of snow through the winter that followed, but he agreed he had got tired of wading through acres of mud.

Listening to them, Lesley felt a pang. When she first went to Raventhorpe paddling about in Wellingtons had been all part of the marvellous sense of freedom she had experienced. After years of academic slog, it had been fun to help bring in the cows or feed a motherless lamb with a baby's feeding bottle. She had tramped the fields with Carne, and gone with him to market. She had drunk halves of bitter in the Red Lion, and listened to the talk about crops and feed stuffs and if she had had to share Carne's attention with the other men, she had cherished the thought that when their bedroom door closed that night, she would have him all to herself for hours and hours and hours . . .

Those were the days before she had Jeremy to care for, when she hadn't had the time to listen to Mrs Radley's continual barbs or care if she ridiculed her naïve attempts to accomplish some task Carne's mother tackled without effort. She had been free to come and go as she pleased, and only as her pregnancy began to weigh her down was she forced to spend more and more time in the house. She had a hard time having Jeremy, and although Carne had insisted she have the child in the maternity hospital in

Thirsk, it was weeks before she felt physically strong again. Another black mark against her, she thought now, remembering how Mrs Radley had jeered because she had not been able to feed the baby, and maintained that she had had her four children without complications and been out in the fields again with them sucking at her breast. Lesley hadn't disbelieved her. Carne's mother seemed capable of anything. Except liking her . . . Maybe if he had married the daughter of one of the local farmers, she would have felt differently. Marion Harvey had obviously expected to occupy Lesley's position, and even though Carne was married had lost no opportunity to spend time with him. They had had a different set of values from her, Lesley decided coldly. No doubt Marion was still around. The wonder was that Carne hadn't asked for a divorce before this and married her. Unless she had married someone else, of course. That was always possible. And it didn't necessarily mean there would be any drastic change in their association. Marion had lived on a farm all her life. She knew all there was to know about the relationship between the male and the female of the species. No doubt she'd learned it first hand from an early age, thought Lesley spitefully, remembering how Marion and Mrs Radley had laughed when she had asked why the bull spent its days tethered while the cows ran freely in the pasture. No, she had been all wrong with Carne. She was city born and city bred and, in Mrs Radley's opinion, too soft to cope with life in the Yorkshire dales.

She dragged her thoughts back to the present as Carne's cool eyes turned in her direction. 'Are you ready?' he asked quietly, and she inclined her head. She doubted she would ever be, but she looked at her mother and murmured: 'I'll see you later.'

'Don't hurry back on my account,' Mrs Matthews averred, apparently determined to be awkward, and Lesley's twitching lips scarcely formed a smile as she walked towards the door.

She walked quickly along the corridor to the lift, and to her relief it was already occupied when it stopped at their floor. She and Carne squeezed inside, and the door closed behind them creating an absurd intimacy that would have been suffocating without the presence of other people.

It was an escape to cross the entrance hall and emerge into the cool evening air. It was pleasantly warm now, not so humid as it had been earlier in the day, and Lesley allowed the scarf to fall loosely about her waist and over her forearms.

Realising she could not continue leading the way as she had been doing, she looked up at Carne as they reached the bottom of the apartment building steps, eyebrows raised in polite question. There was no sign of the station wagon she saw apprehensively, and she was very much afraid her mother was going to be right about him leaving it at his hotel.

'I've booked a table at a small Italian restaurant in Greek Street,' he informed her. 'Do you feel up to the walk, or shall I hail a taxi?'

There was a challenge in his eyes, and before she could help herself Lesley exclaimed: 'I can walk!' although her feet quailed at the anticipation of nearly a mile in the sandals she was wearing. She should have accepted her mother's advice for the good sense it was instead of assuming she was just being obstructive, but she determined that Carne should not suspect she had doubts.

By the time they were passing the railed environs of the British Museum, she was almost ready to concede defeat. Carne had kept up a blistering pace, striding along beside her with a complete disregard for the length of her legs when compared to his. She was not a small girl, but she was not an Amazon either, and she was not accustomed to walking much anywhere, although she would never admit it to him. She should have dressed in a sweat shirt and cords and Wellingtons, she thought resentfully. Obviously he imagined he was out on the Fells, and that his dinner would get cold if he didn't get back in time to eat it!

Gritting her teeth, she forced herself to keep pace with him, but she was never so relieved than when St Giles Circus hove into view. The towering mass of Centre Point was ringed by traffic lights, and they crossed with a crowd of other people to go down Charing Cross Road.

Antonionis was not a new restaurant, but Lesley had not been there before. She couldn't help wondering how Carne had known about it, but she had no intention of asking. It was no business of hers how often he chose to come to London, but she did wonder if he came alone.

The lighting in the restaurant was low and discreet, the tables set between trellises twined with climbing shrubs and vines. There was music provided by two men who played an assortment of instruments between them, but mostly arranged for piano and guitar.

Seated on the low banquette that made a horseshoe round the table, Lesley surreptitiously slipped off her sandals and pressed her burning soles against the coolly tiled floor. She closed her eyes for a moment, the relief was so great, but opened them again hurriedly when Carne asked: 'Are you feeling ill?'

'What?' Lesley's response was guilty. 'Oh, no. No.' She swallowed. 'I—er—I've never been here before.'

Carne studied her slightly embarrassed features for a few moments longer, and then transferred his attention to the white-coated waiter hovering at his side.

'We'll have the wine list,' he said, speaking with the cool assurance Lesley had always admired. 'And bring us two Campari and sodas to be going on with.'

'Yes, sir.'

The waiter withdrew and Carne's attention turned back to Lesley. But she had had a few seconds to compose herself, and to shuffle along the velvet seat so that now they were seated at right angles to one another. It was easier than facing him, although she was conscious that if she moved her feet too recklessly they would touch his ankle.

'So,' he said, toying with his dessert fork. 'Isn't this civilised?'

Lesley decided there was nothing to be gained by antagonising him again, and forced a faint smile. 'Isn't it?'

'And how is he?'

'How is who?'

For a moment her mind had gone blank, but Carne patently didn't believe her. 'Well. I don't mean Lance Petrie,' he retorted coldly. 'Or your latest boy-friend.'

'I don't have a boy-friend!' exclaimed Lesley indignantly, and then cursing herself for allowing him to get under her skin, went on more evenly: 'I'm sorry, I was miles away. You mean Jeremy, of course.' She paused, striving for control. 'Well—he's fine. So far as I know.'

'What do you mean? So far as you know?'

Lesley sighed. 'I mean I get a weekly letter from him. All the boys are expected to write home at least once a week. It's not much of a letter usually,' she reminisced, forgetting for a moment to whom she was speaking, and then recovering again, added: 'He was all right when he wrote a week ago.'

Carne's eyes glittered in the muted lights. 'It never

occurred to you to suggest that he might write to his grand-mother and me, did it?' he demanded, and she flushed.

'You showed no interest in him,' she exclaimed defensively, and ignoring his angry oath, finished: 'Besides, it's possible the boys at school imagine his parents live together. Jeremy might not have confided in them. And writing two letters would create—difficulties.'

The waiter reappeared with their Camparis, and accepting the wine list Carne said they would order their meal in a few minutes. The waiter smiled, and after bestowing a warm glance on Lesley, departed once more.

Carne cradled his glass in his hands, warming its frosted surface with his fingers. 'What have you told him about me?' he asked at last, and Lesley chose her words carefully.

'He—he doesn't remember you at all . . .'

'You haven't told him I'm dead, have you?' Carne demanded savagely, and she hastened to reassure him.

'No. But—well, since he's been old enough to understand, you've not been around, and—I don't suppose he's had time to formulate any ideas.'

'Did you tell him you walked out on me?'

Lesley concentrated her attention on the ice in her glass. 'I—I told him we weren't—happy together. Until recently, he was just a baby, remember?'

'So as soon as he was old enough to start asking questions, you packed him off to boarding school.'

'No!' Lesley was horrified. 'What else could I do?' Then, realising this could lead to all kinds of alternatives, she added: 'I went to boarding school myself.'

'I didn't,' remarked Carne dryly.

'No, well, that's nothing to do with me.'

'I know. But what kind of education my son gets is to do with me.'

Lesley took a gulp of her Campari and soda before asking doubtfully: 'What—do you mean?'

Carne hesitated a moment, and then shook his head. 'Later. Right now, let's get back to why we're here, shall we?'

'Mother's—illness?'

'Among other things.' Carne frowned into his glass. 'Look, Lesley, I think I ought to come straight to the point.'

'To the point?' she echoed faintly.

'Yes.' He paused. 'I want you to agree to letting Jeremy come and spend his summer holidays at Raventhor——'

'No!' She interrupted him before he could finish. 'No, I won't agree to that, and you have no right to ask me.'

'No *right*?' He made a sound of annoyance. 'My God, you're a great one to talk about rights! Well, okay, maybe I have let you have your own way for so long that you've come to the entirely inaccurate conclusion that I intend to let you go on that way. But deep down, you must have known that sooner or later I'd want my turn!'

'Your *turn*!' She forced herself to return his cold gaze. 'Jeremy's not a toy you can pick up or put down at your leisure.'

'I know that.' Carne glanced round as if afraid their raised voices were being overheard. 'But I was fool enough to believe that given time you'd come to your senses.'

'To my senses?'

'Stop repeating everything I say, for heaven's sake!' He took a deep breath. 'Lesley, you might as well know, I've been corresponding with your mother ever since you left Ravensdale.'

Lesley gulped. 'Corresponding with—oh!' She broke off abruptly as she realised she was repeating him yet again. 'Checking up on me?'

'In a manner of speaking. I wanted to be sure you were all right. You and Jeremy both.'

Lesley stared at him contemptuously. 'You can't seriously expect me to believe that.'

'Whether you do or whether you don't is immaterial,' he retorted. 'But like I keep telling you, Jeremy is my son. I haven't forgotten that, even if you have.'

'Oh, I haven't forgotten,' she exclaimed bitterly. 'What part has my mother been playing? Watchdog? A spy to let you know if I went out with another man so that you could gather a case to take Jeremy away from me? *Your* mother would like that, wouldn't she? She was always jealous that there was one person who preferred me to her!'

'Stop it!' His jaw had hardened angrily. 'I expected you'd have grown out of such childish ideas by now. Why bring my mother into it? This is between you and me.'

'Oh, no.' She shook her head. 'It was never *just* between you and me. She was always there to take your side, to assure you that you could do no wrong.'

'Oh, God!' He raked back his hair with long impatient fingers. She noticed it was longer than he used to wear it, brushing his collar at the back, but still as thick and straight as ever. He had never worn a hair dressing, and she had loved to slide her fingers through it . . .

Now, he controlled his features, and said: 'The fact remains that I stayed out of Jeremy's life when it seemed that you could do most for him. Coming down to London to see him wasn't a satisfactory arrangement, and you know it. So I decided to wait——'

'Like a vulture!' she muttered, but he ignored her.

'—until he was older and could be told the truth.'

'And you think that time has come?'

'I don't know. All I know is, your mother wants out of

the present arrangement. So far as I'm concerned, the boy can come for a holiday and nothing need be said. It's up to you.'

Lesley's mouth felt dry in spite of her steady sipping of the Campari and soda. 'Let—let me get this straight,' she got out unsteadily, 'you're saying that if I let Jeremy come to you for the holidays, you're prepared to take it no further?' She put a confused hand to her head. 'What *do* you intend to tell him?'

'I've told you, that's up to you.'

'Oh, no.' Lesley moved her head slowly from side to side. Raventhorpe meant Mrs Radley, and Mrs Radley would not be prepared to say nothing. 'Your mother would see that Jeremy was told exactly what a poor substitute for a wife I had been. Somehow she'd make him believe that I was the guilty party.'

'And weren't you?' demanded Carne violently. 'I didn't walk out on you—take your son away from you!'

Lesley shifted uneasily on the banquette. 'You know, this is getting us nowhere . . .'

'I agree.' He finished the liquid in his glass, and summoned the waiter. 'I suggest you consider the alternatives. Either you give me the temporary custody of my son willingly, or I'll take you to court and prove that I can give him a better home life than you ever could!'

CHAPTER THREE

THE menu was not large, but it covered many of the traditional dishes of Italian food. Lesley chose a chilled fruit juice and lasagne, although she doubted she would be able to eat any of it. Still, the waiter was not to blame for her present predicament, and she hoped he would not blame her if she did not do full justice to the chef's ability. Carne ordered spaghetti with a bolognese sauce, and then studied the other diners indifferently as Lesley sought to open the conversation again.

She would not have believed he could present her with such an ultimatum. Either . . . or . . . How could he be so dogmatic after all this time? For over two years now, she had had complete charge of Jeremy's welfare. He couldn't opt out like that and then opt in again just because it suited him.

Clearing her throat, she said: 'I—I don't want this to degenerate into a slanging match, Carne, but I doubt a court would approve of your abandoning Jeremy for more than two years . . .'

'Damn you, I did not abandon him!' he exclaimed, turning to glare at her. 'I've told you. I corresponded with your mother. I was aware of what was going on.'

'Then why did you let me send him to school? Why didn't you step in before he started his education?'

Carne sighed. 'Last year—last year there were problems.'

'How convenient!'

'No, it wasn't convenient at all, as it happens.' His mouth

43

tightened. 'But what we're talking about right now is this year, these holidays.' He paused. 'What are you afraid of?'

Lesley gasped. 'I'm not afraid of anything.'

'Then why don't you want me to see the boy?'

'You can see him any time you like.'

'In your presence—I know.'

'What's wrong with that?'

'Everything.' He waited until the waiter had set Lesley's fruit juice in front of her, and then continued in a low voice: 'Let's put the record straight, shall we? You had a hard time having the boy, I accepted that. I also accepted that you found it hard to recover your strength after you got back to the farm. It was a hard winter, I know. It wasn't conducive to recuperation. But I did everything I could. I gave you a room to yourself—I even kept away from you because I knew you couldn't bear me to touch you——'

'That's your story!' she burst out hotly, and he heaved another sigh of resignation. For several seconds he continued to stare at her and then, with a gesture of defeat, he left her to drink the glass of orange juice.

Lesley tried to calm herself. At every turn he was able to disconcert her, forcing her into reckless retaliation, destroying the façade of composure she was trying so unsuccessfully to maintain.

She swallowed the fruit juice and the waiter removed her glass. If he wondered why his two customers should be talking so earnestly one minute and then so obviously estranged the next, he was too professional to show his curiosity, but Lesley sensed the sympathetic looks he cast in her direction.

Realising it was up to her to say something, she murmured: 'How serious do you think my mother's condition is?'

It was an effort to get him to respond to her again, and she could tell by his expression that he knew that as well as she did.

'All heart conditions need to be taken seriously,' he retorted shortly. 'I suppose it depends on the age of the person and how strenuous a life they lead.'

'Well, Mother doesn't have a particularly strenuous life,' Lesley ventured consideringly. 'I mean, she has Mrs Mason come in three mornings every week to do the housework, and I usually prepare dinner when I get home. She doesn't bother with much at lunchtime, unless she's having a friend over for the day, and occasionally she goes out to play bridge.'

'Until Jeremy comes home,' Carne put in dampeningly, and she was forced to concede that this was true. 'Which brings us back to the point of this meeting,' he continued coldly. 'Well? Are you going to fight me?'

Lesley's brown eyes, so unusual with her fair colouring, flickered upward. 'Fight you?'

'Didn't you always?' he retorted. 'God knows why you ever married me! God knows why I was fool enough to ask you!'

The lasagne lay in thick tomato sauce, a meaty filling between thin slices of pasta. Looking at it, Lesley wondered how she had ever imagined she could taste it. She felt sick, and her fork moved it sluggishly round her plate. It even made a sickly sound, and she pressed her lips together and looked anywhere but at her plate.

Carne didn't appear to be particularly hungry either. He was only picking desultorily at his spaghetti and then, noticing she wasn't eating, he said dryly: 'They're going to think there's something wrong with the food, you know. You don't have a plastic bag in your pocket, do you?'

It was the least aggressive thing he had said to her since they met that afternoon, and unaccountably Lesley's eyes filled with tears. It had all been too much. The problems that morning, coming home and finding Carne there, and now this ultimatum . . .

With a gulp, she dragged her handkerchief out of her bag and getting to her feet looked around desperately for the ladies' room. She had forgotten she had taken her sandals off, however, and when she tried to put them on, she found she couldn't. Half sobbing, she rummaged under the table, and this brought Carne to his feet, too, and the waiter to see if anything was wrong.

As Lesley struggled into her sandals, hiding her face beneath the level of the table, Carne explained that nothing was wrong exactly, the lady simply wasn't feeling too well, that was all, and several notes exchanged hands as Lesley blew her nose and used the excuse to keep her head down as she hobbled across the floor behind Carne.

Outside it was just beginning to get dark, and lights were appearing in store windows and cars were turning on their sidelights. The tall skyscraper blocks of offices and apartments winked with intermittent illumination, and here and there a coloured bulb gave an illusion of festivity.

The first thing Carne did was summon a taxi, and Lesley made no protest when he ushered her inside. 'Why didn't you tell me you couldn't walk in those things?' he demanded disgustedly, as she limped to her seat, and she stared down unhappily at her hands.

'I didn't want you to think I was incapable of walking,' she replied in a low voice. 'Besides, it was taking them off that did it, not keeping them on.'

Carne's hard profile revealed his disbelief, but he made no further comment about her sandals. 'So,' he said, as the cab joined a line of others heading for Shaftesbury Avenue, 'have you decided what you're going to do?'

Lesley made a helpless movement of her shoulders. 'I don't have much choice, do I?'

'You'll let me have him?'

Her lips tightened. 'Temporarily.'

'What's that supposed to mean?'

'You used the word—temporary custody of your son, you said. Well, I don't have any choice—this time.'

'*This time?*' His brows drew together. Even in the filtered light from the neon lighting outside she could see his perplexity.

'Yes.' She clenched her fingers tightly together. 'You hold all the cards at the moment, I can see that. I can't fight you, and you know it. But—but if things were different, if I had a home to offer him . . .'

'What do you mean—a home?' His mouth drew into a thin line. 'Are you thinking of trying to divorce me? Of marrying again?'

Lesley held up her head. 'That would be quite a solution, wouldn't it? I could fight you on your own terms then!'

Carne uttered a frustrated sound. 'All this talk of terms— and fighting . . .' He shook his head. 'For God's sake, Lesley, why should I have to fight for what's legally and morally mine?'

'Oh, morals, is it?' Lesley's temper was briefly dispersing the gloom and despondency that had gripped her in the restaurant. 'You'd know a lot about them, of course.'

Fortunately the glass screen was between them and the driver, and the diffused lighting kept their faces in shadow. But Lesley sensed his interest by the way his eyes kept moving to the rear-view mirror and she moved as far into her corner as she could, staring out blindly at the busy streets.

After her last little outburst, Carne had said nothing, and

as the busy thoroughfares gave way to the quieter squares
of Holborn, her nerve began to give out on her. They would
reach St Anne's Gate in a few more minutes and once she
got out of the cab who knew when she would see him again.

'What—what will you do?' she ventured at last, and his
eyebrows lifted.

'When does term end?'

'Thursday week—that is, a week on Thursday.'

'The fifteenth, then.'

'Is it? Yes, I suppose it must be.'

'How does he get home?'

Lesley hesitated. 'By—by train. To Paddington. I—I
meet him there.'

'I see.' Carne frowned, and then the taxi was drawing up
at the block of flats, and the driver swung open the door for
them to get out.

Lesley followed Carne on to the pavement, expecting him
to bid the driver to wait. But he didn't. He paid the fare
and then, seeing her surprised face, remarked: 'I *can* walk!'
before guiding her towards the entrance.

As they waited for the lift, Lesley wondered what else he
wanted to say. She felt sick and drained inside, unable to
look beyond the holidays, contemplating what might happen
if Jeremy should find he preferred Ravensdale to London.

When she would have rummaged for her key in her bag
and opened the flat door, however, Carne's hand on her
wrist stopped her.

'Wait,' he said. 'There are things that need to be said
before we join your mother.' He saw her eyes jerk to his
hand and released her. 'Like, for instance, I want you to
come to Raventhorpe, too.'

'What?' Lesley's face went even paler than before. 'But
you just said——'

'—that I didn't want to spend all my time with Jeremy in your company—yes, I know. But you're forgetting something. Jeremy hasn't seen me for over two years. It wouldn't be fair to either of us to expect us to—take up where we left off as though nothing had happened.'

Lesley moistened her upper lip. 'You really think I might agree to come to Yorkshire!' she exclaimed. 'I have a job. That's what all this is about, or had you forgotten?'

Carne leaned against the wall beside her. 'You also have holidays,' he pointed out. 'Which, your mother tells me, you take when Jeremy is at home. Why shouldn't you take a week of that holiday at Raventhorpe? If not for mine then for Jeremy's sake.'

Lesley moved her head determinedly from side to side. 'No.'

'Why not?'

She stared at him with incredulous eyes. 'You ask me that?'

Carne straightened. 'I should have thought, after your impassioned appeals to me to let you care for our son, that you'd welcome a week spent in his company. Or are you prepared to spite yourself and wait until Christmas in the hope that he won't want to come back to Raventhorpe again?'

Her composure crumpled. 'You're a cruel swine, Carne Radley!'

'Practical,' he corrected her grimly.

Lesley shifted restlessly from one foot to the other. 'And what will your mother say?' she taunted. 'Aren't you afraid she'll think you're trying to persuade me to come back?'

'Oh, no!' Unwittingly, she had caught him on the raw, and suddenly his hands were gripping her shoulders, forcing her round to face him. 'No,' he said again, looking down into her resentful face. 'She won't think that. She knows exactly how I feel about you!'

'Does she?' Lesley refused to let him see how he had hurt her, and out of the depths of her humiliation came the words to exacerbate his already uncertain temper. 'Does she know that holding me like this makes you tremble?' she asked contemptuously, turning her eyes to the white knuckles that showed through the brown skin. 'How you fight to disguise the fact that I can still arouse you just as I always did? Does she know that, Carne?'

His hot breath was expelled into her face, faintly scented with the odour of Campari. The hands gripping her shoulders tightened convulsively and the blood drained out of her arms, leaving them numb. He was fighting desperately to control the desire to shake her until she was as weak and helpless as a broken stem, but beneath the mask of frozen fury something else was stirring. She saw it in his eyes, in the tiny flames that licked along the chips of black ice, in the twisted sensuality of his mouth; and she felt it in the feverish heat from the body that leapt the space between them to bring a wave of perspiration out all over her.

'You little bitch!' he muttered, his eyes dropping to the low vee between her breasts. 'What do you want from me? *Blood?*'

'Is that possible?' she got out, and then his mouth was crushing hers, bruising her lips against her teeth, forcing her mouth open.

His hands dropped to her waist, jerking her against him. Her thin dress was no barrier to the throbbing pressure she could feel between them and her hands groping to push him away lingered against the ta muscles. So many memories rose to blank out the ang sion in his eyes, and although she knew his strongest e that moment was hatred, she couldn't prevent her body from moulding itself to his . . .

It was eight years ago, and while Lance had been outlining the proposed questions he intended to ask in the filmed interview which was to follow, Lesley had stood and shamelessly watched Carne, stirred as much by the muscles that moved beneath his brown skin as by the arguments he made in favour of an independent farming treaty. He was twenty-six at that time, broader then than he was now, but marriage had fined him down. Compared to Lance, whose bulky frame seemed pallid by comparison, he was younger, stronger and definitely attractive, with an unconscious earthy sexuality that had excited Lesley's susceptible senses. She had never known anyone with such dark eyes before, and encountering those eyes upon her had been aware of her own instantaneous response. He had been aware of it too, she had known that, and the faint humour in the smile he gave her after the interview was over had both tantalised and irritated her. She didn't want to be attracted to a farmer, she had told herself contemptuously, forcing herself to think of all the intellectual people she met in the course of her work. But Carne was not unintelligent, and over the lunch his mother had reluctantly provided for the television crew in the kitchen of Raventhorpe, he had demonstrated his ability to hold his own with the best of them. That fact, combined with his good looks and disturbing personality had made Lesley's preconceptions seem rather weak and childish.

Even so, she had been prepared to dismiss him as rather conceited and arrogant until he offered to show her round the farm before she left. Lance and his technicians were reloading the equipment, but she did not ask his permission before eagerly agreeing, which made a mockery of her pre-

tence of indifference. Carne showed her the milking shed
and the stables, the mare with her young foal, the Friesian
cattle which he told her held the record for the best milk-
producing herd in the district. He showed her the pedigree
bull in his pen, whose beady little eyes drove her a little
closer to her escort, and in the high barn, with its bales of
hay and pitchforks, the tall ladders leading up the loading
gantry, with the sun streaming in through the cracks in the
timbers, in that earth-soaked atmosphere, he had pulled her
into his arms and kissed her.

Until then, she had not known what kissing was all about.
She had been kissed before, mauled even by boys at university, but never had it felt like this; this aching, drowning
feeling, that made her want to wind her arms around his
neck and never let him go. When he had drawn her down
into the hay, she had gone with him willingly, surrendering
herself to him with a wanton abandon which she would
remember with embarrassment later. But right then, it had
seemed the right thing to do.

Of course, it had to be his mother who found them. Fortunately she came soon enough to prevent anything but the
most passionate kind of petting, nevertheless, Lesley had
been hot and shamefaced, not at all amused by Carne's lazy
indifference. His words had sent his mother away, but not
before Lesley had seen the jealous resentment in the older
woman's eyes and felt the whiplash malice of her tongue.

Carne had picked the straws out of her hair and helped
her to straighten her shirt and waistcoat. Her denim suit
showed little harm from its contact with the straw, but she
had felt cheap, and convinced that he imagined she was
easy game for any man.

Lance had looked at her a trifle strangely when she returned to the others, and she wondered whether Mrs Radley

had said anything to him of what she had seen. Then they thanked Carne for his help and wished him goodbye, and Lesley had travelled all the way back to London with an awful sinking feeling in her stomach.

She had never expected to see Carne again, but his re-appearance outside the studios one evening had driven all thoughts of self-recrimination out of her head. He had been waiting for her beside the old Ford convertible he had been driving at that time, and the girls she had emerged with had stared admiringly at the tanned dark man leaning against its bonnet.

'Hi,' he said, and when he swung open the passenger side door, she had not hesitated before climbing inside.

Their courtship had been brief and hectic. They were hungry for one another and the demands of the flesh imposed an almost irresistible strain upon them. But Carne had insisted on marrying her before going to bed with her, and as Jeremy was conceived during the first days of their honeymoon, Lesley was glad she had not tried to persuade him to change his mind. As it was, their first night together had been spent in the hotel in Paris where Carne had booked a suite for the all-too-short week he could spare away from Raventhorpe, and Lesley had come back to her new home convinced that nothing could ever separate them again . . .

She came back to the present to find him thrusting her angrily away from him, wiping blood from his lips which when she licked her own she realised came from her mouth.

'No,' he was saying harshly, looking at the blood on the back of his hand. 'I won't let you make a fool of me again!'

'I? Make a fool of you?' she choked, and he nodded.

'What would you call it?' he demanded. 'Ravensdale is a tight community. Can you imagine what was said after you left?'

'Is that why you want to take me back again?' she cried futilely. 'To prove that you can?'

'If that's what you choose to think,' he conceded, with a cold bow of his head, and as she half turned towards the door it opened, and Mrs Matthews' face appeared.

'Oh, Lesley, it is you!' she exclaimed, and then her eyes moved on to Carne. 'Carne! Are you coming in?'

'Carne was just leaving, Mother,' declared Lesley, brushing past her, but when she would have left them, his voice halted her:

'Thursday,' he said. 'Thursday the fifteenth. What time is the train?'

Lesley hesitated. 'Three—three fifteen,' she admitted unwillingly. 'Why?' She forced herself to meet his gaze. 'You can pick him up here.'

'No.' He shook his head. 'I'll pick you up here before meeting the train.'

Mrs Matthews looked perplexed. 'You're talking about Jeremy?' she asked. She looked at her daughter. 'Lesley, what's going on?'

'You should know,' muttered Lesley, and then relenting added: 'Carne is taking Jeremy for the holidays. Just as you wanted.'

'And Lesley is coming, too. For a week,' Carne stated, daring her to contradict him. 'To help the boy get settled in.'

'You are?' Even Mrs Matthews looked surprised at this, and Lesley pursed her lips.

'I don't have much choice, do I?' She took another step and then looked back at Carne. 'The last week—the last two weeks of his holiday. Can he come back here? I—I'd like to have some time alone with him.'

Carne shrugged. 'We'll discuss it later,' he observed non-committally, and not waiting to wish him goodnight, Lesley disappeared into the living room.

Her mother found her in her bedroom, standing before the long mirror of her wardrobe, tugging a brush through her hair.

'Well?' she said challengingly. 'Did you have a pleasant evening?'

'No.' Lesley shook her head.

'But you've agreed that Jeremy should spend some time with his father. I'm glad about that.'

'I haven't agreed to anything,' replied Lesley shortly. 'I was presented with an ultimatum. But I expect you know about that. As you and Carne have been corresponding!'

'He told you?' Her mother nodded.

Lesley put down the brush and unzipped her dress. 'Do you mind leaving me alone now? I'd like to go to bed.'

Mrs Matthews hovered uncertainly by the door. 'It is for the best, dear,' she murmured persuasively. 'Try and see it that way.' And when Lesley didn't reply: 'How do you think Jeremy would feel if he grew to a man without even knowing his father? I mean, you never know. He might have blamed you. Boys will be boys, you know. It's not like having a daughter, is it? Boys are much more—much more——'

'Independent?' Lesley's mouth tightened. 'Yes, I know. Lucky boys!'

But after her mother had left her, so too did her attitude of control. With a sob of despair, she sank down on to the side of her bed and buried her face in her hands. What a situation she had got herself into! But not by her own doing. Not by her doing at all. Her mother had planned this. Even if she wasn't well, there was no excuse for her going behind her daughter's back and writing to Carne, and

Lesley couldn't help wondering whether this idea hadn't been introduced before Mrs Matthews became ill. She remembered too well how impatient with Jeremy her mother had been at Easter, how eager to get him out of the flat and away from the cluttered bric-a-brac of its rooms. Of course, she was not a young woman, but she was not old either, though she had an old woman's fanaticism for the valueless objects she had collected over the years. If only she had realised, Lesley thought now. She would have made other arrangements—somehow.

In bed, between the cotton sheets, her thoughts irresistibly shifted to Carne and that amazing scene in the corridor. It had been an accident of genius to turn the tables on him like that, although in the all-concealing darkness she conceded it had almost been her undoing. What had put that particular weapon into her hands? How had she known that he would not reject her with the contempt that could shrivel her soul?

With trembling fingers she traced the swollen scar on her lips where his mouth had forced them against her teeth. A shiver of alarm slid along her spine. She had forgotten how aggressively Carne could hold her, how rough his touch could be. But she hadn't forgotten the feel of his hard body, she remembered now, sliding her hands down over her breasts, provocatively pointed beneath the cotton nightshirt, to the smooth line of her thighs. It was more than five years since they had slept together, but she could recall the feel of his body close to hers in the early morning. She hadn't forbidden him her bed, he had chosen to sleep elsewhere, but no one could entirely destroy those memories.

Rolling on to her stomach, she tried to sleep, but it was impossible. There was Jeremy to think about, her darling Jeremy, who soon now was to learn that there was another world besides the one he had always lived in. Another world, where mating wasn't a rude word, and women worked alongside their men instead of playing bridge and giving tea parties. What would he make of that world? What would he make of his father? And his other grandmother . . .

CHAPTER FOUR

PADDINGTON STATION was crowded with a mixture of holiday makers and commuters, and parents there to meet their children from the Taunton train. Standing by the booking office, Lesley tried not to look too obviously for Carne's tall frame, but it was almost a quarter of an hour since he had disappeared to make a phone call and Jeremy's train was due in five minutes.

Nervous fingers smoothed the skirt of the tan-coloured smock she was wearing, and occasionally she lifted a foot and examined the plain wedged sandals with a critical eye. But nothing could rid her of the feeling of imminent disaster that had gripped her ever since Carne arrived at the flat that afternoon, and her anxiety for his return owed more to the distraction of his presence than a desire for his company.

Shifting her bag from one hand to the other, she wondered for the umpteenth time whether she ought to have warned Jeremy what to expect. But what could she have said? *Surprise, surprise, Daddy's going to take you to his home for the holidays! The father you haven't seen for three years, and can hardly remember, is trying to take you away from me!* Over-dramatic, perhaps. Her throat tightened. But how could you introduce such a topic in a letter? Instead, she had contented herself by telling him that they were going to spend part of the summer holidays on a farm. She had not explained that the part she would spend would be much shorter than his. That could come later. It had, however, irritated her to realise that in spite of her resentment towards Carne, it would have been even harder if he had not insisted on her accompanying them. But that didn't make it any easier for her.

'Sorry to be so long. All the phones were occupied.'

Carne spoke right behind her, his breath stirring the strands of hair moistened by the anxious dampness at her nape. Lesley swung round, impatient that she had not seen his approach, aware that his presence was still too much of a liability to give her any peace of mind.

'I was beginning to think you'd had cold feet,' she declared through tight lips, and the corners of his mouth curved down.

'Like you, you mean?' he countered, and her nerves stretched.

'Did you make your call?' she asked, determining not to rise to his baiting, and after a moment he nodded.

'Eventually,' he agreed, and she realised he was not going to tell her to whom he had been speaking.

Looking away from his mocking countenance, she encountered the gaze of a woman who was regarding her with apparent recognition, and who now took the opportunity offered to approach them.

'Mrs Radley?' she queried politely. 'It is Mrs Radley, isn't it?'

Lesley cast a swift awkward look at Carne and then agreed. 'That's right.'

'I thought so.' The woman, who appeared to be in her early thirties, included Carne in her encompassing smile. 'I remember seeing you here in March. My son pointed you out to me. Mark Morrison.'

Lesley cleared her throat, thinking furiously. 'Mark? Mark Morrison? Oh—oh, yes. Mark.'

'I thought you'd recognise the name,' said the woman

comfortably, obviously unaware that Lesley was still as confused as ever. 'Mark and Jeremy are such good friends. Mark's always talking about him.' Her gaze fastened itself on Carne's lean face. 'And you must be his father. I believe Jeremy's always talking about you.'

Lesley only just managed to disguise her gasp of amazement in a cough, but Carne weathered the shock with remarkable composure. His politely controlled features registered nothing but interested approval, and only his eyes narrowed perceptibly, the short thick lashes concealing his true feelings.

'Indeed,' he replied now. 'Good things, I trust.'

'Well, of course . . .' Mrs Morrison appeared flustered. 'I mean—well, naturally Jeremy's very proud of you.'

'Is he?' Carne remained amazingly unruffled. He smiled. 'You know how boys exaggerate.'

Mrs Morrison flushed. 'Boys of any age like to feel proud of their fathers,' she averred. 'And naturally, as you haven't been present at any of the school functions, Jeremy wanted to make it clear that you weren't neglecting him.' She tempered this rather veiled criticism with another ingenuous smile. 'But I understand. It isn't always possible to plan ahead in your business, is it? I don't expect your schedules can be organised to include school speech days and sports days, can they?'

Carne exchanged a look with Lesley, and then shook his head. 'No.' His faint smile was exactly right, showing suitable satisfaction, yet gently appealing for sympathy. 'Nevertheless, I do know—Jeremy's propensity for over-dramatisation . . .' He paused and looked at Lesley with lazy eyes. 'That's one characteristic, however, I can't take the credit for.'

His smile took the sting out of his words so far as Mrs

Morrison was concerned, but Lesley gritted her teeth as the other woman's laugh tinkled lightly. 'Oh, Mr Radley!' she exclaimed coyly. 'You're so modest!' Then she sobered. 'But I wish my husband had been here to meet you. He adores flying, and meeting a genuine airline captain . . .'

This time Lesley's gulp of disbelief would not be denied, but she quickly changed it to a hoarse: 'Isn't this the train?' and to her relief the Taunton express rumbled slowly along the platform.

'Oh, so it is!' Mrs Morrison sounded almost disappointed, but the sight of her son hanging dangerously out of one of the carriage windows sent her hastening away with only a brief word of farewell.

Left alone with her husband, Lesley felt totally incapable of handling the next few minutes, a feeling which was not tempered by Carne's rasping: 'Did you tell him to say that?'

'*No!*' Indignation came to the rescue once more. 'Good lord, as if I would!' She made an impatient gesture. 'Don't be so silly!'

Carne frowned as the train squealed to a halt. 'Don't you think you ought to go and look for your son?'

'Oh! So he's *my* son now, is he?' Lesley tossed her head, but she soon gave in as a stream of boys, both large and small, began to swarm past the barrier, lugging heavy suit-cases behind them.

As she moved forward, she was aware of Carne behind her, tall and attractive in his mud-coloured Levis and matching shirt. She wondered what Jeremy would think of his father, and wished with all her heart they had never encountered Mrs Morrison, with her predispositions of his character.

She saw him almost at once, a smaller boy among a group

of taller ones, tugging his suitcase with evident difficulty, his cap stuffed carelessly into the pocket of his blazer. Her present involvement with Carne made her see him with new eyes, she realised reluctantly, and while Jeremy might never have recognised his father, his father could not fail to recognise him. Apart from the fact that his school-cut hair was much shorter than Carne's, their features and colouring were so similar. The same dark hair and eyes, the same easily tanned skin. Where Carne was lean and muscled, the boy was almost slender, but he was tall for his age, and moved with the same light athletic tread. Unlike his father, he was not particularly clean, she noticed impatiently, and his tie was half unfastened and twisted round his neck. The uniform grey shirt had collected a number of smutty marks *en route*, and the creases in his grey-and-purple striped blazer were not enhanced by the fact that the sleeves were already short on him. Another new blazer, thought Lesley anxiously. However would she afford it?

Jeremy had seen her and was waving energetically, apparently taking no notice of the man behind her. He probably thought it was some other boy's father, Lesley fretted, glancing round at Carne and noticing the unusual lines of strain around his nose and mouth, and then Jeremy had handed in his ticket to the collector and was reaching up to give her a swift, half embarrassed peck on the cheek.

' 'Lo, Mum,' he grinned, handing over his suitcase with his usual disregard for her femininity, and then jerking it back again as Carne's hand came to take it. 'Hey . . .'

'Jeremy, this is your father!' Lesley burst out recklessly, and then wished she hadn't as Jeremy stopped dead and stared up at her disbelievingly, while the waves of school-boys continued to wash about them.

Carne took the suitcase from Jeremy's now-unresisting

hand, and urged the boy forward. 'Come on,' he said. 'The car's outside. We're creating an obstruction.'

He strode ahead, making a way for them to follow, and Lesley took Jeremy's hand and pushed him forward. 'My father?' he said, almost to himself, and then looked at the man ahead of them. 'My father?' He transferred his attention to his mother. 'My *real* father?'

'Yes. Your real father,' declared Lesley shortly. 'Do hurry up, Jeremy. People are trying to get home.'

Jeremy obediently quickened his step and they emerged into the sunlit station yard. Carne had managed to park in a side street just a few yards from the entrance, and he was already turning the corner as they appeared.

But Jeremy let him get out of sight and then turned to Lesley urgently. 'What is he doing here? Mum, why has he come to meet me? You didn't tell me he was staying with Nanna.'

'He's not,' said Lesley, choosing her words with difficulty. 'Oh, love, I can't explain now. It will all come right, you'll see.'

Jeremy hesitated. 'Has he come back to live with us? Are we going to be a proper family again?'

'Well—no.' Lesley sighed, and as she did so Carne reappeared, standing at the street corner, regarding them impatiently. 'Darling, come along. Daddy's waiting. He'll tell you what it's all about.'

'But I don't want him to tell me,' objected Jeremy. 'I want you.'

'Yes, well——' Lesley urged him forward. 'We're coming,' she called to Carne. 'Pick up your feet, darling. Trudging like that wears out the soles.'

The station wagon was hot after standing in the sunshine for almost half an hour. Carne had left the doors and windows open as he waited for them to join him, but still it was unpleasantly stuffy inside.

'Why couldn't we have taken a taxi to Nanna's flat?' asked Jeremy mutinously, pulling his tie into an even more untidy corkscrew. 'I like riding in taxis.'

'You'll get used to riding in this,' retorted Carne, speaking to his son for the first time. Then: 'How are you, Jeremy? Have you had a good term?'

Jeremy didn't immediately answer, and Lesley, seated in the front beside Carne, glanced round encouragingly. 'Have you, darling?' she asked, forcing a smile, and the boy hunched his shoulders.

'It was all right,' he muttered, clearly not happy about this new state of affairs, and Lesley's heart bled for him.

The congestion of the traffic was such that for a time Carne was occupied in negotiating the maze of one-way streets and traffic signals. Lesley kept giving Jeremy encouraging smiles, but his face remained mutinous and sulky, and she guessed he was as anxious as she was about the future. But what else could she have said? she justified herself. To introduce Carne any other way would have only made for complications later. Even so, she sensed Carne was not pleased either, and she wondered if he was letting what Mrs Morrison had told them reflect on his opinion of his son.

St Anne's Gate was blessedly quiet and as soon as the car had stopped, Jeremy had the door open and had hopped out on to the pavement. But as he darted away towards the doors of the apartment building, his father's voice stopped him:

'Jeremy! You've forgotten your case!'

The boy turned, obedience to the tone of voice stronger than his desire to escape. 'Mum will bring my case,' he muttered in a low voice, but Carne shook his head.

'Women don't carry cases,' he replied pleasantly. 'But if it's too heavy for you, I'll carry it.'

'I can manage,' mumbled Jeremy, and came and pulled the case out of the back of the station wagon.

Lesley looked angrily at Carne as Jeremy struggled up the shallow steps, but her husband's expression was bland. 'Isn't that rather childish?' she demanded in an undertone, as Carne closed and locked the car. 'I always carry his case.'

'I know,' he said flatly, and followed his son up the steps.

The journey up in the lift was the most uncomfortable Lesley had ever experienced. Even travelling alone with Carne had not been as tense as this, and Jeremy's pursed lips could not disguise the fact that his chin was wobbling.

Mrs Matthews had seen the station wagon from the windows and opened the door as they came along the corridor. This time Carne had taken command of the suitcase leaving his son free to go and meet his grandmother. 'Jeremy!' she cried, hugging him warmly, and watching the rapturous welcome her mother gave him Lesley felt an angry pang. It was as if Mrs Matthews was disclaiming all knowledge of the arrangements her daughter had unwillingly made with her husband, as if the decision to involve Carne had been Lesley's alone, and she had played no part in it.

In the flat, it was almost as stuffy as in the station wagon. It was a particularly hot day, but windows created draughts, or so Mrs Matthews always maintained, and in consequence the dining room was rather unpleasantly redolent with the smell of the pickled onions lying in their dish of vinegar. A special tea had been prepared by Mrs Mason, but the housekeeper's culinary skills never ran beyond ham and salad, squashy sponge cakes and plates of tinned fruit and jelly.

Even so, Jeremy was pleased, and his automatic: 'Ooh, butterfly cakes!' more than made up for the housekeeper's lack of imagination.

'Won't you sit down, Carne?' Mrs Matthews ushered her son-in-law to the head of the table, and Jeremy's brief excitement died beneath childishly lowered brows.

Mrs Mason, a matronly woman in her early fifties, brought in the teapot and they all seated themselves. Lesley, examining the fatty ham on her plate with a jaundiced eye, wondered what the housekeeper thought of this unusual little gathering, and then her mother's words brought her head up with a snap.

'And has Mummy told you you're going to stay on Daddy's farm these holidays, Jeremy?' she asked pleasantly, chasing a pickled onion round her plate with her fork, only to have it fall unheeded to the floor as the boy sprang up from his seat in alarm.

'No!'

'*Mother!*' Lesley was on her feet too, but it was Carne's arm that prevented Jeremy's headlong dash from the room, and his handkerchief that was pushed without compromise into his son's tearful face.

'Mum . . .' Jeremy turned appealing eyes in his mother's direction and Lesley gave him a sympathetic look before turning to her mother again.

'How could you?' she exclaimed. 'How could you blurt it out like that?'

'You did much the same,' retorted Carne without emphasis. 'And besides, it needed to be said.'

'But not yet!' protested Lesley, with Jeremy's reproachful gaze upon her.

'Why not?' Carne was merciless. 'For God's sake, he's not going to the stake! I'd hazard a guess that he may find it more enjoyable than listening to you two arguing all day long!'

'Carne!' Mrs Matthews sounded most offended, and it gave Lesley a rather cheap sense of satisfaction to know that her husband was not entirely deceived by her mother's air of aggrieved innocence.

Jeremy blew his nose on the handkerchief, and then said tremulously: 'What's going to happen to me, Mum? Why are you sending me away?'

'Oh, Jeremy . . .' Lesley felt near to tears herself, and it was again Carne who squatted down beside the boy, holding him gently but firmly between his hands.

'Listen to me, Jeremy,' he said, as the boy tried to squirm away, 'you knew you had a father, didn't you?' The boy nodded unwillingly, and he went on: 'So you must have thought that some day you might see him again.'

'Mum said you hadn't—hadn't time for—for us,' stammered Jeremy resentfully, and now it was Lesley who bore the brunt of Carne's angry gaze.

'Oh, did she?' he said at last, controlling his feelings with admirable restraint. 'Well, that wasn't entirely true. We just felt—your mother and I—that having two homes might be too confusing to a small boy.'

'Two homes?' Jeremy looked already confused, and Lesley exclaimed: 'Let me tell him!'

Carne's glance was denigrating. 'Don't you think you've had long enough to do so?' he demanded, his voice roughening for a moment. Then, when she made no immediate reply, he returned to the boy. 'So—I'm here to take you to my home now. For a visit. To meet your other grandmother.'

'My *other* grandmother?' Jeremy looked anxious.

'My mother,' explained Carne patiently. 'Nanna is your mother's mother, isn't she?'

Jeremy digested this slowly. Then he said suddenly: 'Why haven't you come to see us before? Don't you like us?'

Carne sighed. 'I'm trying to explain,' he said, straightening to stretch his long legs. 'Like I said, Mummy and I didn't want to make things difficult for you.'

'But you've got time for us now?'

'I always had time,' retorted Carne thinly, then, seeing Jeremy's distrust reappearing, he added: 'Yes, I have time for you now.'

'And—and Mummy, too?'

Carne inclined his head. 'And Mummy, too,' he agreed dryly.

Jeremy's face cleared a little. 'Why didn't you tell me?' he demanded of his mother now. 'Why didn't you say you were coming?'

Lesley forced a slight smile. 'You didn't let me,' she murmured reluctantly, ignoring Carne's faintly triumphant air.

Jeremy turned to his father again. 'And you have a farm? A real farm? Does it have cows and horses and pigs? Things like that?'

Carne's features softened. 'Well, it doesn't have planes and hangars,' he remarked dryly, and Jeremy's brightening face suffused with hot colour.

'Why did you say that?' he demanded doubtfully, and Carne raised his dark eyebrows. 'You don't know?'

Jeremy rubbed his nose with his forefinger and shook his head.

'Okay.' When Lesley would have protested, Carne silenced her with a look. 'Now, shall we finish our tea?'

Mrs Matthews was still looking more than a little put out

by what had occurred. 'I think I'd like to go and lie down,' she declared, dabbing her lips with a scrap of lace. 'This—this has all been too much for me.'

'Mother . . .' Lesley turned to her helplessly, unaccountably feeling that all the people she loved were drifting away from her. 'Mother, please don't get upset.'

'Let your mother lie down if she wants to,' remarked Carne, opening the door for his mother-in-law. 'We'll be leaving soon anyway. She knows that.'

Now it was Lesley's turn to look put out. 'Leaving?' she echoed. She shook her head as if to clear her brain. 'I thought we were leaving in the morning.'

'We were,' said Carne easily. 'But I decided the journey would come easier in two parts. That's why I made that phone call this afternoon. I've booked us into an hotel just off the motorway, near Leicester. That way the boy and I will have more time to get to know one another before we get to Raventhorpe.'

Mrs Matthews came back into the room again. 'Your suitcase is packed, isn't it, Lesley?'

'Well, yes, but——' Lesley looked at Jeremy, and then, realising that what Carne had said was true, she nodded defeatedly. 'Very well. If that's what you want.'

Jeremy, who had squatted down at the table again, looked up from his third butterfly cake with a film of cream across his upper lip. 'Are we really going to spend the night at a hotel?' he exclaimed excitedly. 'Hey, I've never stayed at a hotel before.'

'You sound as though you're looking forward to leaving me, Jeremy,' his grandmother remarked with an injured air, and watching her Lesley was appalled at the way she could act as if this whole idea had been nothing to do with her.

Jeremy swallowed the remainder of the cream cake and

looked up guiltily. 'I'm not—honestly, Nanna——'

'Maybe you'll forget all about us when your mother returns to London,' added Mrs Matthews with a sniff, and both Carne and Lesley stared at her in horror as Jeremy's face crumpled once more.

'When—when Mummy gets—gets back to—to London,' he faltered, but now Carne stepped in.

'Finish your tea, Jeremy,' he said sharply, giving his mother-in-law the kind of look he usually reserved for his wife. 'Nanna's upset that you're leaving, that's all. She's not been well, and she can't cope with a lively little boy like you all the time. You need fields to run in, and maybe a horse to ride. Something to burn up all that pent-up energy you're using on those cakes.'

Only one thing had registered with Jeremy. 'A—horse?' he echoed excitedly. 'I might ride a horse?'

'If you're good,' promised his father, with a dry smile. 'Now, have you finished?'

Jeremy fell asleep on the back seat of the station wagon before they even reached the motorway. He was exhausted, and the enormous tea he had consumed in between his bouts of tears and anxiety had added to his natural weariness. Lesley envied him the ability to escape in oblivion. For her part she was nervous and on edge, not at all easy at the way they had left her mother, and even less easy at the prospect of meeting her mother-in-law again. It had all been precipitated by Carne's decision to leave more than twelve hours sooner than she had anticipated, and she felt ridiculously unprepared.

As if sensing her restlessness, Carne took a moment to glance her way. 'What is it?' he asked softly, so as not to disturb the boy. 'Are you worried about your mother?'

Lesley shrugged offhandedly. 'I suppose so.'

'You have no need to upset yourself on her behalf. She's a tough old bird, believe me.'

'You would know, of course.'

He sounded amused. 'Let's say she won't be worrying about you.'

'What's that supposed to mean?'

He shrugged now. 'Nothing.' He expelled his breath on a sigh. 'Isn't it warm?'

Lesley sighed, too, not at all satisfied with his answer but unable to probe further. Instead, she said: 'Jeremy's case will be full of dirty washing. I intended to take his things to the launderette tonight, so they'd be clean for him going back to school.'

'My mother does have a washing machine,' Carne remarked laconically. 'You can use that.'

'Do you think she'll let me?' demanded Lesley bitterly, and then lapsed into silence again as he chose not to reply.

As the miles were eaten up, a little of the tenseness left her. For good or ill, she was committed to spending the next week at Raventhorpe, so there was little point in upsetting herself about it. She must just hope and pray that Jeremy would not adapt too completely to his new environment, or that if he did she would be unselfish enough to accept it. But a tight lump developed in her throat at this prospect and she had to swallow hard to send it away.

She deliberately thought of Lance, and her work at the studios. He had made no bones about her taking her holiday sooner than anticipated, but he had expressed surprise that she was accompanying Jeremy to Ravensdale.

'I have no choice,' she had tried to explain, briefly outlining Carne's ultimatum to her, but Lance had not seen it that way.

'Look,' he had said, 'I don't altogether agree with

Radley, but I do see that he should be entitled to get to know his son. Your going with Jeremy on the other hand is madness! He's not a baby. He doesn't need you to feed him or dress him or change his clothes. He's been at school a year with strangers. What's so different about him spending his holidays in like manner? They wouldn't be strangers long. Not his father and his grandmother!'

'It's different at school,' Lesley had protested. 'He's with lots of other boys, all in the same boat.'

'You're mollycoddling him, Lesley,' her employer had pronounced flatly. 'And what's more, you'll regret it!'

The hotel where Carne had booked their rooms for the night was situated in the village of Amblefold, just a few miles off the motorway. The Falcon Arms was an old world type of inn, with low knotted beams and a wealth of copper and horse brasses. It wasn't until Carne was actually parking the station wagon on the forecourt that Lesley wondered exactly what accommodation he had booked, and indeed, what names he had given.

Jeremy, awakened out of a deep sleep, was tearful again, inclined to cling to his mother's skirt and act much younger than his almost seven years. Carne strode ahead into the reception area, and by the time Lesley and Jeremy appeared, he had signed the register and been handed the keys.

'First floor, numbers 14 and 15,' said the plump-faced woman who had been attending him. 'Do you need any help with your cases?'

'No, I can manage,' replied Carne politely, and gesturing to Lesley to go ahead, he swung the resisting Jeremy up into his arms.

The first room Lesley entered contained twin beds. It was clean and functional, twin green candlewicks matching the long curtains at the windows.

'This will do for Jeremy and me,' she declared, and Carne made no objection as he set the boy down.

'I'll take next door, then,' he said, as Jeremy recovered sufficiently to go and bounce on one of the beds. 'I'll get the cases first.'

By the time he returned, Lesley had discovered that the bathroom was next door to Carne's room, and Jeremy had already succeeded in getting himself locked inside. Fortunately, careful instructions had got him out again, but not before both of them were feeling rather strained. Lesley was sitting on her bed recovering when Carne knocked at the door, and Jeremy opened it to admit his father with the cases.

'Thank you.' Lesley got up rather shakily, but fortunately Carne didn't seem to notice. 'Is—is your room all right?'

'A double,' he responded briefly. 'Is Jeremy going to bed now?'

'Oh, no . . .'

The boy began to protest, but Lesley was adamant. 'Yes,' she said firmly. 'Why?'

'I thought we might have a drink downstairs,' replied Carne smoothly. 'That is, if you feel like one.'

Lesley did. A whisky or a brandy might be just what she needed. Although on an empty stomach, perhaps it wasn't so advisable.

'All right,' she agreed at last, ignoring her son's sulky scowl. 'Just give me fifteen minutes to settle Jeremy down.'

'Fine.' Carne turned to his son. 'Goodnight, Jeremy.'

'G'night.' Jeremy's response was sullen, but for once Lesley didn't worry. He was tired, and so was she. Things would look brighter in the morning.

After Carne had left them, she opened the case that contained the boy's everyday clothes. His school case she had brought because it contained his slippers and dressing gown, and the assortment of games and keepsakes he took with him everywhere. As he had already used the lavatory, she helped him to undress, and then ran some water into the handbasin in the bedroom.

While he washed and cleaned his teeth, she extracted his slippers and dressing gown from the case, in case he needed them in the night, and turned down the bed ready for his use. Curled between the sheets, his face newly clean and his hair darkly tousled, he looked up at her, a thoughtful frown displacing his earlier sulkiness.

'Mum . . .' he said, apparently searching for words to express what he wanted to say. 'Why are you going downstairs with that man?'

Lesley sighed. 'You know. To have a drink.'

Jeremy looked doubtful. 'You wouldn't—I mean—you wouldn't go away, would you?'

'Go away?' Lesley played for time.

'Yes.' He bit his lower lip. 'What did Nanna mean about —about you going back to London?'

'Oh, that!' Lesley tried to sound casual. 'She was just upset, that's all.'

'You're not upset, are you?'

'Me?' She shook her head. 'I was upset when you locked yourself in the bathroom——'

'No, I don't mean that. I mean you're not upset about us going to stay with—with him, are you?'

'Are you?' It was a calculated risk.

He considered it. Then he said: 'I don't know. It's all happened so quickly.'

'I know what you mean,' nodded Lesley fervently.

'We haven't talked about it.'

'We will, darling.'

'When?' Jeremy was troubled. 'Now?'

'No, not now.' Lesley urged him down on to the pillows. 'Probably tomorrow.'

Jeremy blinked. 'Is—is that man really my daddy?'

'Really,' agreed Lesley heavily. 'I wouldn't lie to you, Jeremy.'

'He's not at all like I imagined,' he muttered, shifting restlessly, and Lesley wondered if he was thinking of the airline captain, but she said nothing.

'There,' she said, getting up from the bed. 'Are you comfortable?'

'I'm hot,' replied Jeremy at once, and his mother sighed.

'I'll fold back the blanket like this,' she said. 'Is that better?'

'Can I take my pyjamas off?'

'No.' Lesley tried not to feel impatient. 'Look, take off your jacket. That's right. Now, I'll put it over here so if you feel cold in the night . . .' She broke off. 'Jeremy, you won't get out of bed while—while I'm downstairs, will you? I mean . . .' She hesitated about putting her fears into words. 'Well, you will stay in bed, won't you?'

'Why are you going downstairs?' demanded Jeremy petulantly. 'I want you to stay here.'

'I shan't be long,' Lesley reassured him. 'And you are tired, darling. Your eyes are drooping.'

Jeremy sniffed. 'Are you going to talk about me?'

Lesley sighed again. 'Probably.'

'What about me? Why has he asked us to stay with him all of a sudden? Are you going to marry him again?'

Lesley shook her head. 'In the morning,' she said firmly. 'We'll talk in the morning. And your father and I *are* married. We were never unmarried.' But as she said the words she wondered how much longer that state of affairs would last. She had the feeling that Carne's motivations were not wholly to do with her mother's heart condition, and it could well be that given the prospect of a possible remarriage he was making the first overtures to gain custody of his son.

CHAPTER FIVE

DOWNSTAIRS, Carne was waiting for her in the bar, seated on one of the high stools, talking to the barman. Lesley slipped on to the stool beside him and acknowledging her presence, he asked what she would like to drink. He himself was drinking Scotch, so Lesley said she would have the same, and looked nervously round the lamplit room while the barman served her drink.

It was an attractive bar, small and intimate, with a few tables set about the flagged floor. A huge open fireplace would make it very cosy when the weather was cold, but presently a fan moved overhead, stirring the languid air.

The barman set her drink in front of her and moved away to serve a couple who had just come in, and Lesley flicked a glance towards her husband. He had not changed his clothes, but he looked quite cool and unperturbed while she felt hot and travel-stained. She promised herself a bath later, when that room was free, and sipped her drink silently, waiting for Carne to say something. But apart from giving her a swift appraisal, he seemed loath to speak, and it was she who finally said:

'I hope Jeremy goes to sleep. He was rather restless.'

Carne looked at her then, the dark eyes as aloof as ever. 'You worry too much about him. Children are remarkably resilient.'

'It was you who insisted I accompany him to Raventhorpe,' she reminded him shortly, colouring as Carne's eyebrows ascended.

'You mean you'd have let him come alone?' he challenged. 'After the way you behaved when I suggested it?'

Lesley looked down into her glass. 'You have an answer for everything, don't you?'

He shrugged, his shirt sleeve brushing her bare arm, causing a ripple of awareness to race along her veins. 'I suggest we try and behave as normally as possible for Jeremy's sake. It's not going to be easy for him, accepting me. But I hope he will—in time.'

Lesley swallowed another mouthful of whisky, feeling her head swim a little as the alcohol surged undiluted into her system. How much time? she wondered anxiously. Was this to be the pattern from now on, or only the bare outline? Would Carne let her retain her guardianship of the boy, or had he in mind the idea to remove him from his boarding school altogether?

Panic made her drink again, more recklessly this time, and when her glass was replaced on the bar it was empty. Carne noticed it, and summoned the bartender again, ordering a refill. Lesley didn't object, although strong spirits had always upset her, but perhaps this evening she could be forgiven, she thought, for trying to dull the sharp edges of her senses.

'Are you hungry?'

Carne's voice seemed to come from a great distance, and she forced herself to concentrate on what he was saying.

'You didn't eat anything of your mother's high tea,' he remarked dryly. 'They do bar snacks here. I suggest you have a sandwich. Unless you'd prefer to go into the dining room. I expect we could have dinner.'

'No, thank you.' Lesley shook her head, although it wasn't a practice she would care to repeat as the room shifted rather unsteadily beneath her wavering gaze. 'I'm not hungry.'

'But you will be drunk, if you go on at this rate,' Carne told her in a low voice. 'I know this has been quite a day for you, but I'm not entirely without feelings myself. Have a sandwich, then we'll both have an early night.'

'I do not want a sandwich,' insisted Lesley, speaking with the careful precision of someone who is afraid the words won't come out right, and Carne finished his own drink and slid off his stool.

'Okay,' he said, and she was disturbed by the angry light in his eyes. 'Goodnight, then.'

'Where are you going?' Suddenly she didn't want to be left alone. The bar was filling up with the evening's trade, and a woman on her own was prey to every would-be Casanova in the district. Lesley didn't think she was up to handling that tonight.

'To my room,' Carne replied now, pushing his hands into the back pockets of his Levis. 'You don't need me, that's obvious. You enjoy your independence, you've told me so. And as Jeremy's in bed and therefore beyond any further overtures on my part, I may as well go and read a good book.'

He inclined his head politely and strode towards the door. The bartender, who had observed their low altercation, came to see if she wanted another drink, but Lesley said no. She wasn't at all sure she should finish the one she had, but she wanted to sleep, so she emptied her glass.

The reception area was deserted when she emerged from the bar, and she lingered for a moment to read the titles of a rack of paperbacks standing near the desk. They were mostly thrillers or the gaudy kind of sexual epics currently heading the bestseller lists, and nothing she saw there appealed to her.

She was turning away towards the stairs when Carne

came in from outside. He was swinging his car keys, and she guessed he had been to check that the station wagon was locked for the night. His eyebrows lifted when he saw her, but he didn't smile, and with an awkward gesture she moved on up the first flight. He had overtaken her by the time she reached the first landing, and dropping the car keys into his pocket, held his hand out for her room key.

She was handing it over when she heard Jeremy crying loud, convulsive sobs that were interspersed with bouts of coughing. She gave Carne an agonised look and then hurried along the corridor, her own unsteadiness vanishing in the anxiety of the moment.

Carne opened the door and they both burst into the room. The sight that met their eyes caused Lesley to halt in dismay, but Carne went past her to lift his son's naked little body clear of the vomit that seemed to be spread all over the bed.

Jeremy was sobbing even more wildly as his father carried him out of the room, and Carne paused to briefly ask Lesley to bring his pyjamas and his dressing gown to the bathroom. When Lesley tentatively opened the bathroom door, Carne had his son in the bath and was quickly washing him down with soap and water. He used the hotel's own towels to dry him, and although Jeremy began to object again when he saw his mother, Carne paid no attention to his tearful pleas.

Lesley hesitated a moment longer, and then, realising the hotel housekeeper would have to be informed, left them to go downstairs again. This time the hotel manager was at the reception desk, and he was most understanding when she tried to apologise.

'These things happen all the time in the hotel business,

Mrs Radley,' he assured her with a smile. 'I just hope the young man will be all right.'

'Oh, yes.' Lesley gave a shudder. 'Too much jelly and too many butterfly cakes,' she averred with a grimace. 'I should never have allowed it to happen.'

'It's easy to be wise after the event,' replied the manager. He picked up the phone. 'I'll have Mrs Scott come and clear the bed.'

Upstairs again, Jeremy's sobs had subsided to a low snuffling, and Carne had already stripped the bed of its sheets. 'Why didn't you go to the bathroom?' exclaimed Lesley, finding relief in anger, but it was Carne who answered for him.

'You'd told him not to get out of bed, apparently,' he remarked dryly. 'Is that right?'

Lesley made a sound of impatience. 'Well, yes, but why didn't you have your pyjamas on, Jeremy?'

'I told you, I was hot,' he muttered defensively, and Carne pulled a wry face.

'At least you won't have them to wash,' he mocked, but before Lesley could make any retort, the housekeeper knocked at the door.

Mrs Scott was round and buxom and thanked Carne for making her work a little easier. 'It's a mercy it's only a single bed,' she exclaimed, with a smile. 'I won't bother making up the bed again tonight, I can do that in the morning. The young man can use the other one, can't he?' She shook a teasing finger at Jeremy. 'You're a wee thing, aren't you, to be needing two beds!'

Lesley gave Carne a shocked look, but Mrs Scott was already bustling out again, the dirty bedding rolled under her arm to drop in the clothes basket waiting outside. The door closed behind her, but before Lesley could formulate her words of protest, Jeremy exclaimed: 'What did she mean? I can use the other bed? That's your bed, Mummy.'

'I know.' Lesley made a helpless gesture. 'I'll call her back . . .'

'I shouldn't.' Carne's words halted her.

'Why not?'

'The booking I made was for Mr and Mrs Radley and son. Do you want to throw doubt in their minds that we're married? Or would you rather that they thought we were splitting up?'

'I'd rather they knew that we were separated!' declared Lesley quickly, and then bit her lip as Carne's eyes moved expressively towards the listening child. 'Well, what do you suggest?'

'I suggest you use the other room,' stated Carne flatly. 'I can sleep on this bed. I don't need pillows and it's very warm.'

'I don't want you to sleep in here with me,' muttered Jeremy sulkily, his chin trembling again, but Lesley didn't see what else they could do. Unless . . .

'I could use that bed, I suppose,' she murmured thoughtfully, but Carne shook his head.

'No.'

'Why not?'

Carne sighed. 'Go to bed, Lesley. I'm too tired to argue with you.'

Reluctantly, she collected her nightdress and toilet things and after kissing a still tearful Jeremy goodnight, she made her way next door. Carne's bed was a double, as he had said, with a yellow bedspread and matching draperies.

The bathroom was empty, and Lesley decided she would take her bath after all. At least the disturbance with Jeremy had dispersed much of the drowsiness she had been experiencing, and the bath water was just cool enough to keep her alert.

Back in the bedroom again, she turned down the bed and slid between the sheets. Apart from his shaving gear and toothbrush, there was no evident sign of Carne's occupation, and she remembered with a rush of heat to her body that he had seldom worn pyjamas. Only once, she remembered him being persuaded to wear some flannelette ones that had belonged to his father. But that had been because he had 'flu, and when she had joined him in the old four-poster they had quickly been discarded.

She turned out the bedside lamp and lay down. It was still light enough outside for her to see quite clearly, and her eyes moved over the fitted wardrobe and dressing table, the armchair by the window where she had deposited her clothes. She would have to go into the other room in the morning and get herself some clean underclothes, she thought, and something other than the smock to travel in. She had a linen slack suit in her case, perhaps she would wear that. It was sophisticated enough to annoy Mrs Radley. Or maybe she would just wear jeans, as Carne was doing. After all, they had annoyed her mother-in-law just as much. Shameless things, Mrs Radley had called them, observing the way they had clung to Lesley's shapely limbs. She hadn't thought that about her son's, thought Lesley with remembered indignation, and his had been equally revealing. But then, she shifted restlessly, Carne was the kind of man who looked good in almost anything. He had that kind of body.

She turned on to her side and tried to compose herself for sleep. She could hear no sounds from the room next door, so obviously Jeremy had had to accept the new arrangements. Was he already asleep? She guessed he would be. He had been tired to start with, and being sick always exhausted him. He wasn't often ill like that, but she guessed bouncing about in the back of the station wagon hadn't helped his digestion, and if she had known Carne intended leaving that evening, she would have made sure he didn't overeat. But he always made a pig of himself when he came home from school, and she knew from experience that school meals were seldom better than adequate.

The rooms overlooked the front of the hotel, and she heard some people emerge and go to get into their cars. The sound of laughter and the firing of the car's engine came clearly through the open window, and on impulse she slid out of bed again and went to close it.

The night air was cool and scented with the fragrance of some stocks growing round the borders of the forecourt. There was no moon, but the sky was a bed of stars, each winking in their turn as her eyes struggled to focus upon them. The slight breeze drifted down the neck of her night-shirt, chilling her refreshed body and bringing a wave of goose pimples out all over her flesh. With a sigh, she pulled the window almost shut and then padded back to bed.

She was pulling her pillow into shape when she heard the gentle tap at the door. She stopped what she was doing and listened, her flesh prickling uncomfortably, and then the tap came again, and Carne's voice beyond the panels called: 'Lesley! Lesley, are you awake?'

The feeling of blind panic left her, and she got quickly out of bed and hurried to the door. Opening it a crack, she whispered: 'What is it? Is it Jeremy? Is something wrong?' But Carne just shook his head and propelled the door inward. He switched on the light and she scurried back to the enveloping shelter of the sheets, staring at him anxiously across the width of the room.

'So you are still awake,' he observed flatly. 'I thought you might be asleep by now.'

'Like Jeremy?' she asked, and he nodded.

'Like Jeremy,' he agreed.

'What do you want?' she exclaimed, in a low voice, and he looked casually about him.

'I thought of asking the manager for a spare key, but I decided that might not be a good idea,' he remarked. 'There was no need in the circumstances.'

'But what do you want?' she persisted, and his eyes ran over the taut nervous shape of her under the covers.

'Well, I could say I came for my jacket,' he drawled, and her eyes darted round the room.

'It's not here,' she protested, and he nodded.

'I know. I just said, I could say that.' He picked up her tights which had fallen on to the floor with the drift of her passing and deposited them on the chair. 'I wanted to talk to you.'

'To talk to me?' She shook her head. 'We talked earlier.'

'I know we did. Not very satisfactorily, as it happens.'

'There's not a lot to say.'

'You think not?' He wandered aimlessly round the room. 'I don't agree.'

Lesley drew up her knees and wrapped her arms around them. 'You're sure Jeremy's asleep?'

'Oh, yes, I'm sure.' A faint smile crossed his lips. 'I watched his eyes close. He didn't much care for me being there, but exhaustion's a great leveller.'

Lesley bent her head. 'Thank you for—well, for dealing with everything.'

'That's what fathers are for, aren't they?' He came to stand beside the bed. 'That—and other things.'

'Carne!' She looked up at him unhappily. 'Why did you come in here? It wasn't for your jacket—and it wasn't just to tell me about Jeremy . . .'

'Would you believe—to share this bed?'

'To—to share this bed!' Lesley's face suffused with colour. 'But you can't do that!'

'Why not? We're still married, aren't we?'

'Yes, but——' She broke off helplessly. 'I don't want to sleep with you.'

'Why not?'

'You know why not.'

'You flatter yourself,' he retorted politely. 'I said I wanted to share your bed. I didn't say anything about making love to you.'

Lesley shrank back against the pillows. 'Then why should you——'

'Why should I suggest it?' His lips twisted. 'It's going to be a long night. And probably quite a cool one. Why should I freeze to death in the next room, with you occupying a bed like this all to yourself?'

'I might have known you had this in mind when you offered me your bed!' she declared bitterly. 'All right, get in. I can't stop you. But keep away from me, that's all.'

Lesley was turned on to her side when Carne's weight depressed the springs at his side of the bed. The light was extinguished and he adjusted his length comfortably beside her. Then there was silence.

Not surprisingly, Lesley found it no easier to sleep than before. It was more than five years since they had last shared a bed, and longer than that since he had made any overtures towards her. How could she be expected to behave as if he wasn't there, when every nerve in her body cried out to her that he was?

'Relax!'

Carne's voice in the deepening darkness broke into her tense reverie and she shifted a little further away from him.

'I am relaxed,' she lied, but he clearly didn't believe her and she heard his grunt of impatience.

'Go to sleep,' he said. 'Like you used to do. I know how you feel, but believe me you needn't worry. You froze me off years ago.'

'I froze you off?' Her echoing of his words was indignant. Then she endeavoured to compose herself again. 'Is that your excuse?'

The mattress beneath her depressed sharply as he shifted his weight. 'I don't need an excuse,' he retorted harshly, and her shoulders hunched almost defensively.

The silence that followed was broken only by Lesley's uneven breathing, a staccato sound punctuated by an occasional sniff which seemed to irritate Carne.

'Don't you have a handkerchief?' he demanded at last, and she burrowed under the pillow for the tissue she had thrust there earlier. She blew her nose loudly, and then subsided again, more tense than before but perceptibly quieter.

Again there was silence in the room and after a while Lesley decided Carne had gone to sleep. With a sigh of relief, she turned on to her back, only to start violently when he said: 'Can't you lie still?'

'I—I thought you were asleep,' she stammered, aware that there was only inches between them now, and he made a sound of frustration.

'Asleep!' he muttered. 'My God, what do you think I'm made of? *Stone?*'

'I don't know what you mean——'

'Don't you?' He turned his head on the pillow to look at her. 'I thought you did. I thought that was what all this was about.'

Lesley swallowed. 'I'm sorry if I keep disturbing you, but I'm not used to sleeping with—with anyone.'

'Meaning I am?'

Lesley licked her dry lips. 'Well, I—I should think you might be more experienced at it than me,' she declared unsteadily.

'Would you?' He turned completely on to his side, and his warm breath fanned her face. 'Yes, well, I suppose that's a fair comment. You lost all interest in sex after Jeremy was born, didn't you? While I——'

'How—how dare you?'

Lesley almost choked, but his tone remained infuriatingly mocking. 'You can hardly lie in bed with a man and say a thing like that,' he pointed out wryly. 'You really are unique, you know, Lesley. A Victorian anachronism in twentieth-century guise!'

'Why, you—you——' Her only recourse was to get out of the bed, but almost before the thought had formulated itself, and certainly before she could put it into action, he had forestalled her, rolling over and straddling both her legs with one of his. It meant that the whole weight of him was imprisoning half her body, and one hand was gripping her waist just below her rib-cage.

'Don't be a fool!' he was saying impatiently, trying to keep it impersonal, but the feeling of his muscular legs against hers made Lesley aware of her own body's betrayal.

'I—I want to get up,' she insisted, and the draught of her words came back on her warmed by the heat of his throat. His arm was raised above her head to support himself, and the raw male smell about him brought back memories she would rather forget.

'You can't,' he said now, his tone thickening slightly. 'I won't let you.'

'You're a brute!' she protested, and then, untruthfully: 'You're hurting me!'

'No, I'm not,' he denied grimly. 'But don't tempt me.'

'To—to do what? Satisfy that overriding ego of yours?' she taunted, and even in the gloom she could see the anger flashing in his eyes.

'You're very reckless, considering the circumstances. Aren't you afraid my—er—overriding ego will compel me to take what's still legally mine?'

'You said you wouldn't touch me!' she exclaimed, and he made a sound of contempt.

'You shouldn't be so trusting,' he declared, and thwarted her efforts to fight him with an ease that terrified her.

'What—what are you going to do?' she cried, and felt his hand move from her waist to close over the ripe fullness of her breast. The nipple was hard and his fingertips probed it delicately, while she shifted desperately beneath him.

'How interesting,' he murmured, and her breath came on a sob.

'All right!' she burst out tremulously. 'You can force me to respond to you. I can't help that. But it won't stop me from despising you for the liar that you are!'

'A liar now, am I?' he muttered savagely, and then, with a harsh word of denigration, he flung himself away from her and out of the bed, putting the width of the room between them.

It was so unexpected that Lesley lay there for seconds after he had removed his weight, her body still maintaining its attitude of supporting him. It was crazy, but she felt a moment's regret, a brief sense of privation that filled her with alarm before, trembling, she drew the covers over her shaken limbs. She curled up in a ball and stared at the tall figure outlined by the window. She could see now that he was not naked, but the dark trunks he wore did little to disguise the powerful muscles of his body, and a wave of despair swept over her at the realisation that by hurting him, she was hurting herself too. He had his back to her, and she pressed her lips tightly together against the urge to appeal to him. She had done nothing to be ashamed of. He had come in here with the sole intention of spending the night with her, and whether or not he had intended anything more was really immaterial. He had mocked and humiliated her, and he deserved her censure.

He looked round at last and she saw him trying to adjust his eyes to the gloom. He seemed to be searching for something, and she was unable to remain silent any longer.

'What—what are you doing?'

'I'm looking for my clothes,' he replied flatly, and she realised he had control of himself again. He came towards the bed and found his pants. 'Go to sleep.'

'But what are you going to do?'

'What do you think?'

'You can't go back to Jeremy's room.'

'Why not?'

Lesley sat up. 'Carne, please! I—won't you stop this stupidity? I mean—come back to bed. Let's just get some sleep.'

He paused. 'What kind of an invitation is that?'

She bent her head. 'I just want us to be—civilised.'

'Civilised?' He expelled his breath on a long sigh. 'Yes, I guess that is what you'd call it.'

'Then . . .'

He raked back his hair with a weary hand. 'Lesley, you're not going to sleep with me beside you, are you?'

'Why not?'

'I don't know. I just know it.'

'I will. I will.' She tried to see his expression in the darkness. 'I'm tired. Why shouldn't I sleep?'

'I don't know.' He shook his head. 'Look, I don't think——'

'*Carne!*'

'All right.' Anger snapped for a moment. 'But remember, this was your suggestion, not mine!'

She nodded and he drew back the covers once more. She tried not to stiffen as he made himself comfortable, and then it was silent again. Even the air in the room seemed curiously still and only the distant whistle of a train re-assured her that they were not the only wakeful people in the world.

Eventually, Carne's deep breathing told her that he had gone to sleep, and she released the tight muscles at her neck. Her head sank more deeply into the pillow and a tired lethargy began to drift over her. It would be morning soon enough, she thought without enthusiasm, and she could do without dark circles round her eyes to meet Carne's mother again. Carne's mother! She stretched her legs more easily. At least at Raventhorpe there would be no question of her sharing a bed with her husband . . .

She opened her eyes reluctantly to find that the curtains she had drawn the night before were not as thick as she had imagined. Snatches of sunlight were forcing their way be-tween the woven threads, filling the room with early morning brilliance.

She knew immediately where she was, which proved she had slept more shallowly than she had thought, and she didn't need to turn her head to know that Carne was in bed beside her. The warmth of his body was a tangible thing behind her, and when she tentatively moved her arm, her hand brushed his thigh.

He seemed to be still asleep and she wriggled round carefully, trying not to disturb him. But the tail of her cotton nightshirt was imprisoned beneath him, and as she tried to detach herself his eyes opened. The thick lashes hid their expression, but his tongue emerged to lick his dry lips and one long-fingered hand slid lazily through the tumbled thickness of his hair.

'What time is it?' he asked, yawning, and obediently she consulted the square watch on her wrist.

'Six-thirty,' she told him nervously. 'Did I wake you?'

He moved his head slowly from side to side. 'I was awake half an hour ago. I guess I must have fallen asleep again.'

'You were awake?' One hand went selfconsciously to her tangled weight of hair. 'Was I snoring?'

'Not to my knowledge,' he responded shortly. 'Did you sleep well?'

'Did you?'

'I slept,' he agreed non-committally. Then: 'I suppose I'd better get up.'

Lesley glanced awkwardly at him. 'About last night, Carne, I—I'm sorry——'

'Forget it.' His tone was flat as he turned and thrusting back the covers got to his feet. 'It looks like being another hot day.'

Lesley sat up, knees drawn to her chin, but without the encompassing folds of covers. Carne, who had picked up his pants, gave her an impatient stare.

'I don't need an audience!' he declared shortly. 'Look, forget about last night. It won't happen again.'

'Oh, Carne . . .' Her lips curved upward, only to describe a reverse curve as she encountered his warning gaze. It was madness, a small voice inside her warned, but still she continued to look at him, her eyes moving compulsively over the hard planes of his face, the taut curve of his jawline, the arrow of hair that darkened his chest and drew her eyes to the lean muscularity of his hips.

'Have you seen enough?' he demanded at last, his voice hoarse and tormented, and she coloured hotly, tearing her eyes away and plucking nervously at the bedspread. 'Can I put my clothes on now?'

'I'm sorry,' she said inadequately, but uttering a tortured imprecation, he dropped his pants and seized her shoulders and hauled her up out of the bed. She was crushed against him as his mouth bruised hers, parting her lips with passionate expertise. Still only lately woken from sleep, she had had no time to construct any defences against him, and besides, the pressure of his hard masculine limbs made her curiously weak.

The sensuality of his kiss was changing, and his hands had slid beneath the nightshirt, seeking and finding the surging fullness of her breasts. Somehow he had unfastened the buttons, and it slid from her shoulders just as he pressed her back against the pillows, his own urgent body bearing hers down.

'Carne . . .' she managed to say once, but it was hardly a protest, her own hands spread against his smooth skin.

'I didn't plan this, Lesley, but God knows, I'm a man, not a saint!' he groaned, and lips moistened at her breast sent the blood spinning dizzily through her head. Passion wasn't savage, she thought incoherently, but sweet, sweet . . . And then the caressing arousal of his hands swept even these thoughts into the maelstrom of sensual oblivion . . .

CHAPTER SIX

CARNE was already dressed when Lesley summoned the energy to lift her head from the pillow. She was lying on her stomach, and she turned slowly, drawing the covers protectively over her. He was fastening the belt of his Levis, and looking at his withdrawn features, she would never have believed that only minutes before he had been making love, his eyes glazed and passionate, his body trembling in her arms. Now he looked cool and detached, a thoughtful frown causing a deeply drawn cleft between his brows.

He saw her watching him, and his mouth drew down at the corners. 'Are you all right?'

Was she all right? Lesley could have laughed at the question, but it would have been hysterical laughter. And yet she couldn't altogether blame him for what had happened. She might not have been able to stop him, but the most galling thing was that she hadn't even tried. On the contrary, if she was honest with herself, she would acknowledge she had encouraged him, and the consummation of their lovemaking had been as rapturous and satisfying as in the early days of their marriage. Further, it had matured, like wine, and its heady full-bodied fermentation had swept away her fears and inhibitions and left her wantonly wanting more. But Carne must never know, he must never have that power over her, she thought, struggling for self-possession, and with a sudden pang she realised how careless she had been. After Jeremy was born, she had insisted on practising birth control, but she had given that up years ago after leaving Raventhorpe, and now here she was taking the most enormous risks without a shred of protection . . .

'I said—are you all right?'

Carne had come to stand beside the bed, and her cheeks flamed at the possibility that he might be able to read her thoughts. But if he did, he read them wrongly, and his voice was cold as he added:

'For God's sake, Lesley, you'd think I'd violated a vestal virgin! We were man and wife for almost two years, you know. There's no need to look at me as if I'd destroyed your innocence. I know I shouldn't have done what I did, but— well, you didn't exactly turn me off!'

'Did I turn you on?' she asked facetiously, but it had a hollow ring and he knew it.

'Get dressed!' he advised, consulting his watch. 'It's almost eight. Or do you want your son to think you slept in the raw?'

'Jeremy!'

For a brief moment in time she had forgotten all about him, and guilt caused her to throw back the covers without really thinking what she was doing. Colour burned in her face again, but Carne resignedly turned his back and she snatched up her dressing gown and made for the bathroom.

When she came back, Carne had gone, but her suitcase was occupying the end of the bed. She rummaged through it eagerly, anxious to find out what was going on next door, and came up with clean panties, jeans and a sleeveless cotton vest. It was too hot for more formal gear, she decided, so Mrs Radley would have to accept her as she was. After all, her son had, she thought emotively, and that had always been the thing Mrs Radley could not swallow.

She had to knock to gain admittance to the other room and Jeremy himself opened the door to her dressed in his underwear. He looked none the worse for his upset the night before, and grinned when he saw his mother.

'There you are,' he said. 'We've been up ages.'

Lesley's eyes went past him to Carne leaning indolently against the window and she wondered how he had explained his absence when Jeremy awakened. 'Have you, darling?' she said now, transferring her attention back to her son. 'Why aren't you dressed, then?'

Jeremy's face fell. 'Oh, do I have to wear my uniform again? I thought you said you'd brought my jeans!'

'Oh, I have. I have.' Lesley made an apologetic sound. 'I'll go and get them. They're in my case.'

'Good-oh!'

Jeremy grinned again, apparently not at all perturbed at being left with his father, and Lesley, pulling his jeans and tee shirt out of the suitcase, thought rather maliciously that she wouldn't be at all surprised if he started calling Carne Daddy before the day was out.

'I'm going to see the bull!' he announced, pulling on his jeans without his father's disdain for an audience. 'Have you ever seen a bull, Mum? Have you ever been really close to one?'

'No!' declared Lesley, rather shortly, folding his pyjamas and dressing gown. 'Did you clean your teeth this morning?'

'Of course.' Jeremy was offhand, more concerned with the things he planned to do than with those he had done. 'Mum, do you know how to drive a tractor? I'm going to learn. Did you know a person could drive a tractor when they're only sixteen, not seventeen, like for a car?'

'You're a long way from sixteen yet,' retorted his mother quellingly, and sensed Carne's mocking gaze upon her.

'I don't think she's interested, Jeremy,' he drawled, with irritating candour. 'Are you hungry? Shall we go downstairs and order breakfast while your mother finishes packing?'

Jeremy hesitated, his obvious desire to learn more about the farm conflicting with his loyalties towards Lesley. 'I—er—what do you think, Mum?' he asked at last, shifting the decision on to her shoulders, and Lesley made a gesture of indifference.

'Go, if you want to,' she said curtly, and then, seeing his troubled face, added: 'Yes, go along. I shan't be much longer myself.'

With the cases packed again, Lesley examined her reflection in the mirror of the vanity unit. Her brown eyes, so unusual with her colouring, were dark and slumbrous, her cheeks faintly pink with the rasp of Carne's jaw. An imprint near her right breast could have been the mark of his thumb, but it was not distinguishable as such, or so she hoped.

She must have been crazy, she thought in disbelief. All those months when she had lived at the farm and Carne had not laid a hand upon her. And now, in the space of two weeks, he had thrown her hitherto uneventful world into a turmoil. She recalled the events of the night before with painful incredulity. How could she have invited him to share her bed? No doubt he had planned the whole thing, and she had gone along with it with all the naïve obedience of a schoolgirl.

She sighed. No, that wasn't strictly true. He couldn't have arranged for Jeremy to make himself sick, or been sure that she would go along with his suggestion to sleep in his bed. If only she hadn't had those two whiskies, she thought with bitter hindsight. Maybe then she would have felt more capable of handling the situation. And yet, as she left the room and made her way downstairs, she had to concede the depressing truth that it was this morning when she had really betrayed herself.

The dining room was small, but cheerful, and in spite of her nerves, Lesley found she was ravenously hungry. Ignoring Carne's speculative interest, she ate cereal and bacon and eggs, toast and marmalade, and finished it off with several cups of strong black coffee. Carne himself ate with less enthusiasm, and he and Jeremy talked throughout the meal, the boy displaying a warmth towards him that smacked of shared interests. Perhaps Jeremy did need a man in his life, she conceded reluctantly. Would it eventually come to the crux of deciding which of them he needed most?

Such thoughts were not conducive to digestion, but piling into the station wagon for the last stage of their journey, Lesley was more anxious about the welcome she was likely to receive at their destination than worrying over some nebulous time in the future. Instead, she gave in to Jeremy's request to sit beside his father, and herself occupied the back seat, along with some farming periodicals and Carne's leather car coat.

They made good time, stopping for a snack lunch at twelve and pressing on into North Yorkshire. The M.1. gave way to the M.18. which in turn gave way to the A.1. Then, beyond Dishforth, they left the motorways altogether and turned on to the minor roads that led into Ravensdale. After the freedom of two and three-lane traffic, the country roads seemed narrow and twisting, but Lesley found her attention soon caught by the beauty of it all. Climbing up and down, through lushly pastured fields, which in winter could be as bleak and desolate as any place on earth, she recognised the waters of the Ravensbeck reservoir, and beyond, the twisting valley of the Raven that gave Ravensdale its name.

Carne was talking to Jeremy, pointing out Scar Cross and Ravensmoor, Warrengill and Liddesmoor Forest. There was the huge Norman keep of Burnridge a twelfth-century castle largely fallen into ruin, and the ivy-clad ruins of the nearby abbey, destroyed during the reign of Henry VIII. He was indicating the different farmhouses, telling the boy who owned them, but inevitably they reached Kirkby Clough, the nearest village to Raventhorpe, and Lesley felt all the fears and anxieties she had been experiencing crystallise into a hard knot of apprehension inside her.

As if sensing her unease, Carne's eyes met hers through the reflection of the rear-view mirror. There was query there, and some impatience, but mostly the heavy lids concealed their expression, and she guessed he had his own doubts about how she would react if Mrs Radley made things difficult for her. She wondered what his mother would say if she was told that her son had been unable to keep his hands off her. Bitter memories hardened her heart. It would not be received at all well, but maybe that was her defence against Carne. Her lips tightened. It was the first time she had admitted that she might need one.

Raventhorpe was the largest holding in the district—a thousand acres, covering much of the fertile pasture of the valley floor and climbing the limestone terraces to the desolate moorland above. Approximately a third of the land was leased by tenant farmers running sheep on the moorland ranges, but Carne's most profitable income came from his milk yield and the pedigree herd he had improved over the years. At present, he was telling Jeremy, he was experimenting with a breed of French cattle whose milk capacity was greater, and Lesley realised his knowledge of biochemistry had not gone to waste.

Carne drove over a cattle-grid and they were on Radley land, land that had been in the Radley family for more than two hundred years. He was the only son of this generation of Radleys, but two of his sisters had married local men and continued to farm in the district. His eldest sister, however, had married a vet, and they had their practice in the nearby village of Ravenswick. It was this continuation of family loyalties which Lesley had found so hard to accept, although with hindsight she understood that Carne could not have abandoned his responsibilities. Maybe she would never have asked him to if his mother had accepted her. But Mrs Radley had always been opposed to Carne's 'city' wife, and Lesley's desire for independence had flowered.

With the car windows down, the smell of new-mown hay was intoxicating, mingling as it did with the scent of wild thyme and poppies, and the damper scents of the river. The Raven had swept round in a curve to slice through the pasture below Raventhorpe, its banks bright with meadow-sweet and foxgloves, and the fence that edged the paddock was overhung with bindweed and flowering thistle.

Jeremy was enchanted, leaning out of the window eagerly, pointing at the foal that kicked its legs as the station wagon passed. But before he could ask if he might feed the colt later, a horse came galloping across the fields to meet them, its rider waving enthusiastically. Lesley guessed it was a woman because of the hat she was wearing, but not until she drew nearer did she realise it was Marion Harvey. Or was she still unmarried? The hand holding the reins seemed to be adorned with several rings.

Carne slowed and eventually stopped, and Lesley found her teeth were all on edge. It was ridiculous after all these years, but she wished she could have felt installed at Raventhorpe before the other woman made her appearance.

Marion appeared to have no such inhibitions. She reined in her chestnut hunter and climbed down just as Carne got out of the car, and the smile she gave him had all the possessive intimacy of which she was capable.

'You're back,' she said, unnecessarily, and Lesley felt if they had not had an audience she might well have kissed him. 'I saw the car from Maltby Pike.'

Carne turned to his son who had scrambled out behind him, ignoring Lesley's admonishment to stay where he was, and smiled. 'We made quite good time on the motorway,' he said, as Jeremy came to stand beside him. 'But it's good to get away from the diesel fumes, isn't it, son?' and Jeremy nodded happily, pleased with his importance.

'So this is Jeremy.' Marion barely glanced at the car as she spoke. 'What a big boy you are! You were just a baby when I saw you last.'

Jeremy looked doubtful, and glanced round at his mother. But Lesley had assumed a sudden interest in one of the magazines beside her and he had to answer for himself.

'Do I know you?' he asked, and Marion's laugh grated on Lesley's already strained nervous system.

'Do you know me?' she echoed. 'Don't you remember Aunt Marion? I thought we were friends.'

Lesley's lips tightened. That was patently not true. Marion had never had any time for babies, and while she had suggested that when Jeremy was older he might regard her as an adoptive aunt, he had grown to boyhood in London.

While Marion was speaking to the boy, however, Carne took the opportunity to put his head through the car window. 'Don't you think you could stir yourself to speak to an old friend?' he demanded, his eyes dark with impatience, and Lesley felt irritated that he should feel the need to reprove her.

'Miss Harvey is no friend of mine,' she retorted, aware of

his anger, but his: '*Mrs* Bowland!' brought her head up with a jerk.

'She's married?' she demanded involuntarily, but Carne shook his head.

'Widowed!' he corrected coldly, and withdrew.

Widowed! Lesley could hardly believe it. She stared at the other girl, tall, and quite heavily built in the manner of the daleswomen, and simply could not see her married to anyone. Although Marion was a couple of years older than she was, she had always appeared younger, not so much in looks but in behaviour, and her love of horses had curtailed any aptitude for dress sense she might have had. She invariably wore corded pants and checked shirts, similar to what she was wearing now, relying on her forceful personality to attract attention. But married—and widowed! In what—four or five years? It was incredible. What was the name Carne had used? Bowland? *Bowland?* The only Bowland she could remember was old Aaron Bowland, who had farmed High Etherley, the holding at the head of the valley.

Marion was looking towards the station wagon now and Lesley found she was not as immune to attention as she had thought. With a feeling of compulsion, she opened the door and reluctantly stepped out.

'Hello, Lesley!' Marion was irritatingly hearty. 'This is a surprise. Never thought to see you back at Raventhorpe.'

It was a tactless comment, but Lesley ignored it. 'How nice to see you again, Marion,' she returned politely. 'I hear I should offer you my condolences. I'm sorry. I didn't even know you had been married.'

'Oh, that's all right.' Marion regarded her smilingly, but Lesley could see the light of hostility in her eyes. 'Aaron's been dead these six months now. I'm quite recovered from the bereavement.'

'Aaron?' Lesley raised speculative eyebrows at Carne, and his mouth drew down.

'That's right,' he said. 'Marion was married to Aaron Bowland. I thought you knew.'

'How could I?' retorted Lesley sweetly. 'You haven't kept me up to date with every little bit of gossip in the valley.'

Marion's freckled features turned pink, and sensing her husband's silent fury, Lesley turned back to the car. 'Don't you think we ought to be getting on, Carne?' she suggested. 'I'm sure your mother's simply dying to see Jeremy.'

The little group broke up with Marion climbing back on to her hunter and Jeremy coming to scramble into his seat in the front of the station wagon. Lesley resumed her position in the back, and after waving farewell to Marion, Carne got behind the wheel. But he didn't immediately start the engine. Instead, he looked round at Lesley, and she quivered at the look in his eyes.

'Don't you ever make that kind of comment again!' he snapped, his eyes dangerous, but Lesley refused to be intimidated.

'Why not? Wasn't what she said insulting enough to me?' she demanded. 'What's the matter? Were you jealous she chose that old man rather than you? I'm sorry, I didn't know I was treading on any toes!'

Carne swung round, refusing to argue with her further, and noticing Jeremy's anxious face, Lesley was contrite. She had no real cause to be rude to Marion. After all, she had left Carne. Marion was welcome to him, if that was what she wanted. So why did she feel this hateful resentment every time she saw them together?

The gravelled track led up and over a slight rise and there

ahead of them was Raventhorpe. Built of grey Yorkshire stone, its barns and outbuildings circling the house like ramparts, it looked exactly the same as Lesley remembered it. And why shouldn't it? she thought wryly. If it had hardly changed in two hundred years, how could she expect it to change in a mere half decade?

Yet it was different, she acknowledged silently. Carne had installed the most modern kind of milking machinery, and the money he had made had been ploughed back into the land. The house itself had been extensively modernised, and despite his mother's parsimony central heating had been installed, but Lesley knew only too well that in the cold winter months that seemed to last so long in this part of the country, Mrs Radley had only allowed the radiators to be switched on after dark. When Carne came home, Lesley had realised, and she had been too proud to complain.

The station wagon turned into the courtyard before the house and Jeremy jumped up and down in his seat as a pair of old English sheepdogs came bounding round the corner of a barn to meet them.

'Watch they don't knock you over,' Lesley implored anxiously, as her son thrust open the car door and got out, but Carne was out, too, and the dogs only sniffed at Jeremy before welcoming their master.

Lesley gathered her handbag and Carne's jacket, and got out of the station wagon. Well, she thought, looking up at the blank windows of the house, they were here. So where was her mother-in-law?

'Carne!'

The strident voice was familiar and Lesley turned reluctantly towards the door of the house. But the figure leaning heavily on a stick in the aperture was much different from the tall, strong-willed woman she remembered. Mrs Radley had been taller than Lesley, who was not a small girl, and easily twelve stones in weight, with hair only lightly tinged with grey. She had been vigorous and active, belying her fifty-odd years with the power of her personality, contemptuous of anyone who depended too much on other people. The woman now standing in the doorway was thin, almost emaciated, and her dependence on the stick was considerable. Her dark hair had lost most of its colour, and her face was sallow and lined with pain. On a day when Lesley would have expected her to be outside, tending her vegetable garden, she had obviously been indoors, indifferent to the healing rays of the sun. How old was she now? Lesley tried to think. Sixty-three, sixty-four? Something like that. Yet she looked nearer seventy.

Jeremy had looked up from petting the animals and seeing his grandmother, came to stand close to his mother. But Carne beckoned him and reluctantly he followed, with Lesley trailing a little behind.

'Jeremy!' Mrs Radley's voice had softened dramatically. 'So you're Jeremy! Do you remember me?'

Jeremy shook his head, and Carne said: 'He was only a baby, Mother. He didn't even remember me.'

Mrs Radley's eyes moved beyond her son and grandson to rest on Lesley, and the girl had to steel herself to meet that sharp gaze.

'Lesley!' It was a bare acknowledgment, and her daughter-in-law knew in those first few seconds that so far as she was concerned, Mrs Radley would never change.

But something was expected of her, and she moved nearer to say: 'How are you, Mrs Radley?'

Carne's mother's lips thinned. 'I'm well,' she declared shortly, which plainly was not true, but Lesley would not presume to contradict her. 'Shall we go inside?'

Shepherding Jeremy before her, Mrs Radley led the way through the wood-blocked hall into the drawing room. This was a room which had been seldom used when Lesley lived at Raventhorpe, but judging from the newspapers strewn carelessly on the lid of the baby grand piano and the lingering smell of the cheroots Carne sometimes smoked in the evening, this was no longer the case. Which was far more sensible, thought Lesley, exchanging a challenging look with her husband before moving to look out of the window. From here, the sweep of the river was visible, and the whole panorama of the valley spread out before her eyes. It was beautiful, she thought with a curious pang, and then determinedly turned her back on such foolish sentimentality.

Mrs Radley had settled herself on a plum-coloured sofa, one leg supported on a footstool, her stick disposed conveniently beside her. She patted the cushion beside her, indicating that Jeremy should join her, but he chose to return to his mother's side, fidgeting, and staring mutely out of the window.

Mrs Radley accepted the arrangement without comment, and then said shortly: 'I've told Mary to make the tea. She'll bring it in presently. Well? Did you have a good journey?'

Carne, who had been standing inside the door, noticed that Lesley was carrying his jacket. Moving to take it from her, he said: 'The journey was fine!' but meeting his eyes, Lesley saw the flicker of derision that entered them. 'Did Stockley phone about those rams?'

'Yes, yes. I told him you'd gone to London, and he said he'd ring you back tomorrow.' Mrs Radley beckoned Jeremy. 'Come and see your grandmother, child. Let me feast my eyes upon you. You don't know how much we've missed you here.'

Jeremy hesitated. 'He . . .' He glanced towards his father. 'He . . . said I might ride a horse tomorrow . . .'

'*He?*' Mrs Radley sniffed impatiently. 'That's your father, child. Can't you call him that—or Daddy, or something other than *he?*'

'Jeremy hasn't had time to get to know his father yet,' put in Lesley defensively, and bore the brunt of her mother-in-law's scornful stare yet again.

'What time does a child need to get to know his father?' she demanded. 'Unless his mother's filled his head with lies about him?'

'Mother!' Carne spoke sharply. 'Give the boy a chance! This is all new to him, and strange.'

'It shouldn't be,' declared Mrs Radley. 'If he'd been allowed to grow up where he belongs, instead of in some stuffy little flat in London!'

'That stuffy little flat in London is our home!' retorted Lesley hotly, and then, seeing that Jeremy was looking up-set, added: 'Anyway, he's here now. And—and Carne will have plenty of time to get to know him.'

The entry of Mary with the tea was a blessed respite. Lesley remembered the girl who had been at Raventhorpe since she left school. She must be about thirty now, and judging from her ringless fingers, still unmarried. She smiled at Lesley, however, and at the boy, and he responded with a tentative lifting of the corners of his mouth.

The tea tray was placed on a low table before Mrs Radley, and Lesley was obliged to sit on the armchair oppo-site and to accept a cup of the strong brown brew, and one of Mary's parkin biscuits. Jeremy perched on the arm of his mother's chair, nibbling a biscuit, still rather in awe of this old lady who was his grandmother, but who spoke to his mother with such anger in her voice. Carne, Lesley saw with some relief, also accepted a cup of tea, but she guessed he was impatient to go and find Worsley, his head cowman, and the man he left in charge when he was away. She dreaded the moment he would leave her alone with his mother, and then chided herself for the craven coward she was.

Jeremy finished his biscuit and then looked round. 'Where are the dogs?' he asked his father, but it was Mrs Radley who answered him.

'They don't come into the house,' she explained. 'They're farm animals, just like the cows and the sheep. Only Mrs Pepperpot and her brood are allowed to come into the house.'

'Mrs Pepperpot!' It was Lesley who repeated the words, although Jeremy had responded to the name, too.

'I've got a book about Mrs Pepperpot,' he said proudly, and Carne explained that his mother had named the tortoiseshell tabby after Alf Proysen's famous children's character.

'Mrs Pepperpot!' exclaimed Lesley again, amazed to find a lump in her throat. 'I thought she'd be gone by now.'

'She's only seven years old,' observed Carne crushingly. 'Most things last longer than that.'

Lesley's eyes sparkled with unshed tears. 'I thought you might have—have disposed of her after—after I left,' she retorted, unevenly, but Carne shook his head.

'I couldn't wring an animal's neck!' he countered. 'Much as I might have liked to.'

Jeremy frowned, losing the thread of their double-talk, and turning to his grandmother, he said: 'You said Mrs Pepperpot and—and her—her——'

'Brood,' supplied Mrs Radley nodding. 'That's right— kittens. Mrs Pepperpot is rather a naughty pussy. She's always producing lots of little Mr and Mrs Pepperpots, and she brings them into the house and finds homes for them in drawers and linen cupboards.'

'Oh, kittens!' Jeremy's eyes were alight. 'I'd love to see them.'

Mrs Radley got to her feet with difficulty. 'Come along then,' she said. 'I'll show you.'

Jeremy looked dubious then, but his grandmother had taken hold of his hand, and was leading him from the room. He looked up at his father as he passed, as if appealing for direction, and Carne gave him a reassuring nod.

'Go along,' he said. 'I think there are six of them around somewhere at the moment. Mary said she'd left a basket for them by the stove in the kitchen. She'll know where they are.'

Mention of Mary and the possibility of more biscuits in the kitchen brightened Jeremy's anxious little face, and he went happily out of the room.

Alone with Carne, Lesley rose to her feet and faced him. He had not sat down to drink his tea, and stood near the doorway, staring at the painting of the brood mare and her foal which occupied the wall above the fireplace.

'What's wrong with your mother?' she demanded without preamble, and his eyes moved to her as if resenting her interruption of his preoccupation.

'She had a fall—about eighteen months ago,' he replied dispassionately. 'She broke her hip.'

'But——' Lesley spread her hands, 'surely it should have healed by now.'

Carne flexed his shoulder muscles, unknowingly straining the buttons of his shirt across his chest. 'It has,' he stated shortly. 'But there were complications.'

'What kind of complications?'

His eyes narrowed. 'What's it to you? Don't pretend you care. That would be entirely out of character.'

Lesley caught her breath. 'You're a cruel devil, aren't you?'

'No.' He shook his head. 'Just honest.' He turned abruptly towards the door. 'By the way,' he looked back at her, 'you will try and behave civilly towards her, won't you? She suffers a lot of pain, I know, and being confined as she is after the freedom she was used to . . .'

Lesley pursed her lips. 'She hasn't changed that much, Carne. She still detests me.'

His expression darkened ominously. 'Why should you expect anything else? Your behaviour was hardly that of a dutiful daughter-in-law, was it?'

'And what about your behaviour?' Lesley retaliated. 'What would you call that?'

His eyes narrowed. 'Do you mean my past or most recent behaviour?'

She stared at him. 'What do you think?'

'I think you should consider more carefully before jumping in with provocative statements about our relationship. All right. Maybe what happened this morning did shock that petrified little organ you call a heart, but call it retribution if you like. You deserved to be shaken out of that selfish image you've carved for yourself, made to face life as it really is, and not like you would like it to be!'

'How comforting for you to be able to excuse yourself like that,' exclaimed Lesley tremulously, but Carne was unperturbed.

'I don't need excuses,' he retorted coldly. 'What I need is absolution. But not from you. From myself!' and he left her.

The house seemed uncannily quiet after his footsteps had

died away. Private though the flat was, they were never out
of sight or sound of the roar of London's traffic, while here
one could hear the chickens squawking in the yard and the
rustle of the breeze that moved the curtains at the open
window. A bee was trying to find its way out again, but its
humming was hardly a distraction, and the sound of the
cows from the byres indicated that afternoon milking would
soon be in progress. It was all so peaceful, thought Lesley
bitterly, so close to anyone's idea of paradise. If only she
could find a similar kind of peace, but so long as she continued to fight Carne she never would . . .

CHAPTER SEVEN

MARY reappeared as Lesley was pacing abstractedly about the room, trying to find some measure of composure. She stood in the doorway watching her employer's wife for a few moments, and then she said quietly: 'Do you know where you're going to sleep, Mrs Radley? Or would you like me to show you?'

Lesley turned abruptly, pushing back an errant strand of hair with a nervous hand. 'Mary!' she exclaimed with some relief. 'It is nice to see you again.'

'And to see you, Mrs Radley,' replied Mary sincerely. 'My, but that young man of yours is a regular little monkey, isn't he?'

'Why?' Lesley was anxious. 'What's he doing?'

'Oh, nothing much,' Mary was quick to reassure her. 'Just wanted to see those dogs again, he did, so he's got old Mrs Radley chasing after him across stackyard.'

'Mary!' Lesley looked troubled, but the other girl just laughed.

'Don't worry, Mrs Radley won't come to no harm. She's tougher than she looks.' She grinned. 'I should know.'

'Oh, Mary!' Lesley thought how wonderful it was to speak to someone who had no axe to grind against her. 'You're still here anyway. Not married yet?'

'Married? Me?' Mary folded her buxom arms. 'Who'd have me?'

'Now, Mary . . .'

'No, I mean it. Never was one for the men. Too impa-

112

tient, I was. Couldn't do with all that mucking around.'
She paused. 'Found a bloke once, about three years ago,
but he was married, so . . .' She shrugged. 'I'm too fat now.
Too many scones and potato cakes, that's what it is. And
butter, and cream. Always liked good cooking, I did.'

Lesley had to smile. 'Well, I think any man would be
lucky to marry you,' she declared. 'I've never tasted better
pies than the ones you make, and they say the way to a
man's heart is——'

'—through his stomach, I know. But it doesn't follow,
does it? I mean, I reckon, he uses his eyes first and his
mouth second.'

Lesley was actually laughing now, and it was good to feel
the tension dispersing. Accompanying Mary across the
panelled hall and up the carpeted treads of the staircase, she
found herself looking about her with unwilling affection,
realising that some things, like her liking for Mary and her
fondness for the house, could still bring her pleasure.

The house was large and rambling, with four bedrooms on
the first floor, and a further three rooms on the floor above.
There were two bathrooms, one which had been used ex-
clusively by Mrs Radley, and the other which Lesley had
shared with Carne. Only the three of them had actually lived
in the house, the farm workers and Mary and her mother
occupying the tied cottages on the estate.

The room which Mary showed her into now was one of
the spare bedrooms, overlooking the back of the house; unlike the master bedroom, which Mrs Radley had reluctantly
conceded when Carne got married and the room she now
occupied, both of which overlooked the front.

For all that, it was an attractive room, decorated with a
green and lilac striped wallpaper, and a hand-embroidered
satin quilt instead of a bedspread. Someone had thought-

fully placed a bowl of pink and white roses on the chest of drawers by the window, and the incoming draught was conveying their perfume around the room.

Dismissing Lesley's grateful smile, Mary bustled about, flicking a speck of dust from the dressing table here or adjusting a cushion on a bedside chair to her liking. 'It seems to me you could do with a bit of my baking yourself,' she declared, straightening to regard the younger girl with critical eyes. 'Proper skinny, you are. That lass of Harveys' would make two of you!'

'Who?' But Lesley knew. 'Marion? Don't you mean— *Mrs* Bowland?'

'I know who I mean,' retorted Mary, with the familiarity of long service. 'Harveys' lass, she was, and Harveys' lass she'll remain. Mrs Bowland, indeed. What's that they say? Married she may be, but never a wife?' She snorted impatiently. 'Only did it out of pique, she did. Regretted it ever since, that's my opinion.'

'Out of pique?' Lesley was intrigued. She knew she shouldn't be gossiping like this, but she couldn't help it. 'What do you mean?'

But now Mary seemed loathe to continue. 'Oh, nowt,' she said, with characteristic brusqueness, and Lesley knew better than to pursue the matter.

Instead she moved to the window, staring out across the stable yard and the hay barn to the rising fells beyond. Sheep were dotted about the green slopes, patches of grey against the landscape, and she could see a Landrover bumping its way across a field, making for some buildings in the distance. Was that Carne? she wondered tautly. All Landrovers looked the same, she couldn't be sure. Although she guessed he had wanted to put as much distance between them as possible.

Mary still lingered, and turning back into the room, she said: 'I didn't know Mrs Radley had had an accident. How did it happen?'

'Didn't Mr Carne tell you?' asked Mary in surprise, and Lesley felt her cheeks colouring.

'No,' she said carefully. 'No, he didn't. Just that—she had.'

'Oh.' Mary grimaced, and then, apparently deciding there was no harm in elucidating, added: 'Well, she fell down the cellar steps. Two Christmases ago, it was, right on the festive season. Missed everything, she did. In hospital for— oh, something like six weeks.'

'Really!' Lesley was dismayed. 'How awful! But I wonder how she could have done such a thing. She's gone up and down those steps every week for the past thirty odd years!'

'Yes, well—maybe she wasn't being as careful as she normally is. What with all the rows with Mr Carne and all——'

She broke off abruptly, but not before Lesley's curiosity was aroused, and they both stared at one another in discomforted silence.

'I'd better be getting along,' Mary decided, making for the door. 'Where's your luggage and I'll fetch it up?'

Lesley shook her head. 'There's only one case, and it's in the hall,' she said. 'I'll get it myself later.' She paused. 'Mary . . .'

'I've said too much already, Mrs Radley,' Mary declared firmly. 'The boy's room's next door, as you'll probably have guessed, and we still have our evening meal about seven. If there's anything else you want . . .'

Lesley sighed and shook her head. Only answers, she thought depressingly, wishing Mary would confide in her. But after all, why should she? So far as Mary was concerned, she had walked out on her husband for no good reason, and Lesley ought to be grateful that at least she had not turned against her because of it.

Left to herself, Lesley put down her handbag and ran cooling fingers through her hair, lifting it away from her neck and catching sight of her reflection as she did so. Despite her desire to appear calm and composed, there were hectic flags of colour in her cheeks, and her eyes were flecked and troubled. Why had Mary suggested that Marion might have married Aaron Bowland out of pique? What had she meant about Carne and his mother having rows? How had Mrs Radley been so careless, and would she ever recover sufficiently to take up her duties as mistress of Raventhorpe? In those early days, when Lesley had lived at the farm, Mrs Radley had had a finger in every pie in the district. Chairwoman of the Kirkby Clough branch of the Women's Guild, active member of the church council, organiser of the local point-to-point meetings; she had regularly run the cake stall at the agricultural show at Ravensbeck, and entered her own jams and preserves in all the competitions. In truth, her record was a daunting one, and Lesley, newly graduated from university, had known next to nothing about any of the things she held dear. Baking cakes or making jam had been a hit-and-miss affair at best, and she had retired defeated from any contest with her mother-in-law.

Lesley could see now, with the wisdom of experience, that she must have appeared quite useless so far as Mrs Radley was concerned. But then Carne's mother had always compared her with girls like Marion Harvey. The fact that Carne had made a fool of himself over her, as his mother had put it, damned her further in Mrs Radley's eyes, and those occasions when she had come upon them in one another's arms had deepened the scowl of contempt she continually wore in her daughter-in-law's presence. That she was jealous, too, was concealed very well, but Lesley knew she resented the hold she had had over her only son.

Jeremy's room had been newly decorated with strip-cartoon wallpaper, and a bedspread depicting the outline of a motor car. Lesley knew he would love it, and he would also love the pile of toys someone had thoughtfully provided for him. There were jointed army dolls and a helicopter for their use, a car transporter, complete with vehicles, games and jigsaw puzzles and boxes of toy soldiers; a veritable treasure chest of entertainment for someone of Jeremy's age.

Thinking of Jeremy made her wonder where he was, but a swift glance out of the window did not enlighten her. Burt Worsley was talking to one of the other cowmen by the milking shed, but there was no sign of Mrs Radley or her grandson, or indeed of Carne himself.

On impulse, before going downstairs in search of her son, Lesley went to the door to the master bedroom, the bedroom she had used to share with Carne until he had chosen to sleep in the room she was occupying now. The door opened easily on to golden-brown tumble-twist and plain cream walls. Long cream silk curtains moved in the draught from the windows and the figured cream bedspread was turned back to reveal brown sheets. The few prints that occupied the walls Lesley had chosen, but otherwise it was completely different from when she had slept there. Only Carne's brushes occupying the glass tray on the dressing table, and a tie draped carelessly over the square bedpost denoted anyone used the room, and its bare simplicity drove a shaft of sudden pain through her chest. They had been happy, she thought emotionally. But it had all gone wrong . . .

Downstairs again, she found Mary in the spacious kitchen busily shelling peas into a bowl.

'Let me help you,' she offered at once, and Mary hesitated only a second before handing over the chore.

'If you're looking for Jeremy, he's not here,' she announced, moving to the long stainless steel drainer unit, which had been part of the modernisation. 'He's gone over to Barrowside with—with his father. You don't mind, do you?'

'It would be all the same if I did,' replied Lesley, her smile a trifle forced. Already Jeremy was moving away from her, and it was not a good feeling. 'Did he ask where I was?'

'I don't know. They'd gone when I came downstairs,' explained Mary uncomfortably, and Lesley gave her an understanding smile as she seated herself at the long pine table.

'Mrs Radley's in the drawing room if you want her,' Mary added, dropping potatoes into a bowl. 'Young Jeremy does like a steak and kidney pudding, I hope. I thought you could have that, and maybe a piece of raspberry pie to follow.'

Lesley looked up. 'I can see you're determined to make us fat!' she observed ruefully, forcing a light tone, and Mary looked relieved.

'Well, I think you could stand it,' she exclaimed. 'It'll do me good to cook for a family again, and put some flesh on bones!'

Lesley looked down at the pea-pod in her hand. 'Carne's mother's lost a lot of weight, hasn't she?' she ventured, and Mary sighed.

'I'll say this,' she declared, as if coming to a decision. 'There's been a lot of unhappiness in this house since you left, Mrs Radley, and no mistake——'

'*Mary!*' Carne's mother's voice was harsh and grating. 'You talk too much. You always did—and about things you know nothing about.'

Mrs Radley was leaning heavily against the framework of the kitchen door, watching them, and Lesley, looking across at her, wondered how long she had been there.

'I just thought Mrs Carne ought to know how things have been,' Mary retorted now, with no sign of intimidation.

'*Mrs Carne!*' Mrs Radley made it sound like an insult. 'You'd best call her *Miss* Matthews, for that's what she'll be soon enough, I've no doubt.'

'What do you mean?' Lesley had to steel herself to remain where she was, when every nerve inside her was crying out to her to stand up.

'I mean when Carne divorces you, of course,' replied Mrs Radley coldly. 'You must know that's in his mind.'

'I didn't know.' Now Lesley could sit still no longer. 'Carne doesn't confide in me!'

'He doesn't need to, does he?' exclaimed Mrs Radley scornfully. 'There are new laws now, you know. Anyone who can prove they've lived apart for more than two years can apply for a divorce with or without the consent of the other party.'

Mary was looking embarrassed, but Lesley had to pursue it. 'Then why didn't he do it before this? Why didn't he get a divorce?'

'Because of the boy,' retorted the older woman cuttingly. 'Carne's not a complete fool, although where you're concerned I've sometimes had my doubts. He cares for his son, and as soon as your mother wrote and told him you were sending Jeremy away to school, he realised the truth of what I've been telling him for years. You only took the boy away to spite him! You didn't really want the trouble of a baby at all, did you? As soon as he was old enough, you got rid of him.'

'That's not true!' Lesley was white-faced. 'That's not true.'

Mrs Radley sneered, 'Try convincing Carne of that!'

'He had to go to school——'

'But not boarding school.'

'He did. I—there was no one to—to look after him.'

'So you admit it?'

'Mrs Radley, I have a job of work. I have to earn money.'

'If you were so keen on working, why did you give it all up to marry my son? You were never happy here, we both know that. Why the devil didn't you stick to your own kind?'

Lesley's mouth was parched and her tongue felt as if it was glued to the roof of her mouth. She had had arguments with Mrs Radley in the past, but never had Carne's mother displayed her feelings so openly. She was glad Jeremy was not around to hear it. Rows always upset him, and she sensed Mrs Radley would not care what lies she told in front of the boy if she could turn him against his mother.

'I think you ought to ask Carne that question,' she said now, speaking slowly and deliberately, choosing her words with care. 'He asked me to marry him, not the other way about.'

Mrs Radley pressed her thin lips tightly together, and then turned and stumped away down the hall, leaving Lesley's legs feeling absurdly like jelly. She was glad to sink down again into the chair beside the table, and her fingers automatically continued popping pea-pods as if nothing momentous had happened. Mary, still standing disapprovingly by the sink, clicked her tongue and turned back to her task, and for a while there was silence between them.

The appearance of a huge tortoise shell cat, stalking in from the yard, its plume of a tail raised proudly, brought Lesley out of her state of numbed disbelief. 'Mrs Pepperpot!' she exclaimed, although her voice wobbled over the last syllable. 'Oh, Mrs Pepperpot, it's so good to see you again!'

Sinking down on to her knees beside her chair, she gathered the disdainful creature into her arms, but the cat, unprepared for this demonstration, flexed its claws against her bare arm.

'Ouch!' Lesley released her abruptly, but at least the incident had served to banish the foolish emotionalism she had been feeling. 'Still as independent as ever, aren't you?' she exclaimed. 'We must be two of a kind.'

Mary glanced round then, her face revealing her indignation. 'That's right,' she declared. 'Don't you let that old besom scare you away! Frightened of losing her position here, that's all she is. Always has been.'

Lesley looked up, still kneeling on the floor. 'I don't know why,' she said wearily. 'Her position was never in any doubt.' She shook her head and got slowly to her feet. 'She knows I'm only here for Jeremy's sake. Why can't she at least try to be polite?'

Mary looked as though she would like to say more, but discretion got the better of her. 'This sounds like Mr Carne now,' she said, as the low rumble of a motor vehicle came along the side of the house, and Lesley had barely time to wash her hands before Jeremy came bouncing into the kitchen, grinning all over his face.

'Hello, Mum,' he said, sparing a moment to greet her before turning back to the man who was following him. 'I've been for a ride in the Landrover. It was great!'

Lesley managed a faint smile, and then Carne's tall frame

blocked the sun in the doorway, his Levis already smeared with grease. He had rolled back his sleeves and unbuttoned his shirt almost to his waist, and the sweat glistened on his smooth flesh.

His gaze flickered quickly over Lesley, and then moved to Mary. 'Something smells good,' he remarked, reserving his smile for her, and she gave him an answering greeting.

'Steak and kidney pudding,' she said, putting fresh water into the pan of potatoes, 'and don't you say you're not hungry because I shall be very cross.'

'I saw some sheep,' added Jeremy, addressing his mother again. 'And I met Mr Newton who looks after them. We went to his house, and his wife gave me some home-made lemonade. Oh, and some biscuits,' he added guiltily, as Mary pulled a face at him.

'Well, don't you go refusing your dinner, my lad,' she said, but it was only teasing, and he knew it.

'I like steak and kidney pie,' he said shyly, and immediately won Mary's affection. 'The food at school is awful! The potatoes are all lumpy, and they have tapioca! Frogspawn, we call it.'

'Jeremy!'

Lesley called a halt to this particular topic of conversation, but she guessed it was something else Carne would store up to use against her when it came to a discussion of Jeremy's education. But he would not succeed in taking the boy away from her, she told herself fiercely, although not very convincingly.

Dinner was served in the panelled dining room. Lesley guessed this was a concession to their presence. In the old days, they had eaten in the kitchen, more often than not, and Mrs Radley had kept the dining room for special occasions. But like the drawing room, it was no longer sacrosanct, and Lesley couldn't help thinking how much nicer it was to sit at the polished oak table with the whole sweep of the valley visible from the long Georgian windows.

Jeremy was having dinner with them, too, but it was late for him and Lesley couldn't help thinking that Mary's satisfying steak and kidney pie was hardly the best thing for him to go to bed on. She determined to have a word with Carne some time during the following day and ask him whether Jeremy might not have a high tea about five-thirty so that he could get to bed at his usual time of half past seven. But tonight was a special occasion, she conceded, and he was enjoying the feeling of being important. Mrs Radley, seated opposite Lesley across the table, never spoke unless it was to or about Jeremy, and his father was almost as guilty. Lesley herself said practically nothing at all, doing her best to do justice to Mary's cooking and trying not to feel apprehensive of the weeks ahead, when she would not be here.

After dinner, it was Jeremy's bedtime, and Lesley took him upstairs after he had said goodnight to his father and grandmother. He undressed tiredly, the events of the day uppermost in his mind, and he settled down on his pillows still talking about what he was going to do tomorrow.

'Do you think you're going to like it here?' Lesley knew it was an unnecessary question, but it had to be asked, and he nodded eagerly.

'Did you know my—my father owns most of this valley?' he asked, putting his hands behind his head. 'Grandma says there've always been Radleys in Ravensdale. She says it will all belong to me one day.'

Lesley's lips compressed. 'Grandma shouldn't tell you things like that,' she replied severely. 'Little boys have a lot of growing up to do before they decide what they want to do with their lives. You might not like farming when you get older. You might want to be a—a doctor, or an engineer, or—an airline pilot.'

Jeremy's air of self-confidence evaporated. 'You know, don't you?' he said miserably. 'Someone's told you. Who was it? Did someone from school write to you?'

Lesley sat down on the side of his bed. 'It was someone we met at the station yesterday,' she explained. 'A Mrs Morrison.'

'Oh!' Jeremy pursed his lips. 'The Blot's mother!'

'Who?' Lesley stared at him.

'The Blot! Mark Morrison. You know—mark—blot! Get it?'

'Reluctantly,' agreed Lesley dryly. Then she sighed. 'But why ever did you tell him such a thing?'

Jeremy sniffed. 'I didn't tell him, actu'ly. It was Hubbard.'

'Old Mother, I suppose.'

He giggled then, and shook his head. 'No, Hubbard's one of the prefects. We wouldn't dare make jokes about him.' He hesitated. 'It was after sports day, you see. No one came——'

'Darling, I was working!'

'I know that. But—well, after—after the parents had gone, Hubbard and one or two others cornered me and said I was a—a—a basket!'

'A basket?'

'That's what they said.'

'Oh, I see.' Lesley understood only too well.

'They said I didn't have a father, that they betted I didn't even know who he was. I said I did. I said he was too busy to come to a rotten sports day. So—so I made that up, about him being a pilot, I mean. No one else's father was one of them, so I didn't think they'd find out. Now, I suppose they have.' He looked glum.

'Not exactly,' remarked Lesley reassuringly. 'Your father didn't—rat on you, as they say. But I really think you ought to tell them the truth anyway.'

'What truth?'

'Why, that your father's a farmer, I suppose. Or a landowner, at least. Sooner or later, someone's going to find out that he's not an airline pilot, and then your life won't be worth living.'

Jeremy's lips trembled. 'I wish I never had to go back there,' he muttered, and her heart plummeted.

'What do you mean?'

'I hate that place,' he mumbled in a low voice. Then he looked at her. 'Couldn't I live at Nanna's and go to a school in London? I'd be ever so good. I wouldn't be a nuisance or anything, and Nanna would look after me.'

Lesley got up from the bed, pulling the covers straight as she did so. 'I think it's time you went to sleep, don't you?' she suggested gently, bending to kiss him. 'We'll talk about this some other time.'

Jeremy shifted uncomfortably. 'I've got a tummyache,' he complained, and a feeling of impotence swept over her. She no longer felt as if she had any control of the situation, and Jeremy's indigestion only accentuated the forces working against her.

'I've got some milk of magnesia tablets in my case,' she said. 'I'll get them.'

He chewed the tablets while she waited and gradually his discomfort began to subside. When his lids began to droop she tucked him in, said goodnight again and left him. But in her own room, the feelings his helplessness had evoked would not be so easily dispersed. Who, at Raventhorpe, was fit to take care of him? Mrs Radley was so eaten up with jealousy, she would do anything to win his favour; Mary's affection was genuine but because of her position limited. Only his father offered any chance of a normal relationship, but would he use the time to poison his mind against her?

It was an impossible situation, but not one which would be resolved by staying in her room as if she was afraid to share their company. However, when she came downstairs again, only Mrs Radley occupied the drawing room, and Lesley remembered that Carne had often spent his evenings in his study. The sight of the older woman seated on the velvet sofa made her want to turn back again, and in those moments she realised that that was where she had gone wrong in the past. By letting Carne's mother see that she could intimidate her, she had lost the battle before it was waged. But she was older now, and harder, she decided, and as ready as Mrs Pepperpot to defend her rights.

She had changed her clothes for the evening, and the hem of her apricot skirt swished silkily across the carpet. Worn with a cream silk tunic and several gold chains, the outfit was more formal than a shorter skirt without being too dressy, but Mrs Radley, looking up from a tablecloth she was embroidering, dismissed her appearance with a contemptuous stare. Her only concession to the evening had been to change her navy blouse to one of black, and to fasten the triple strand of pearls Carne's father had given her about her stringy neck.

Determining to behave as if the afternoon's contretemps had not occurred, Lesley seated herself on the couch opposite, and crossing her legs, asked: 'Where's Carne?'

Mrs Radley looked up. 'Working,' she replied shortly. 'Making up for all the time he's wasted trailing down to London.'

Lesley forced a smile. 'You really haven't changed at all, have you, Mrs Radley?' she observed dryly. 'Absence hasn't made the heart fonder so far as you're concerned, I see.'

Her mildly sarcastic words caused her mother-in-law to bestow another look upon her, and there was an edge of irritation to her voice as she exclaimed: 'Don't you talk down to me, madam!' which proved she was not entirely unfeeling.

'I was merely confirming what's been blatantly obvious from the minute I stepped from the car!' Lesley protested. 'But I hoped we might be able to come to an understanding.'

Mrs Radley snorted. 'An understanding! Is that the kind of talk you've learned from that television producer you work for? Let me tell you I understand you only too well, and whatever you've come back here for, you're wasting your time.'

It was incredibly difficult to remain unmoved in the face of such opposition, but Lesley ignored the provocative challenge, and went on: 'Whether you like it or not, Carne asked me to come here. He knew Jeremy would find it strange, settling down here with—with virtual strangers.'

'And you didn't object, of course,' sneered Mrs Radley, causing Lesley's hackles to rise in spite of herself.

'Of course I objected,' she argued. 'I didn't want to come here. I knew—or rather, I *remembered*—how you would react to that.'

Mrs Radley sniffed. 'When are you leaving?'

Lesley examined her toenails emerging from the straps of her sandals. 'Next weekend,' she replied evenly. 'As arranged.'

'Next weekend!' Mrs Radley sounded furious. 'But that's over a week.'

Lesley looked up into her outraged fa~~ ~~at's right.

So don't you think it's rather silly for us to remain enemies like this? I mean, that was all right when I was young and foolish enough to be intimidated by you, but we're all older, Mrs Radley, and life's too short to waste our energies in futile confrontations.' She paused, allowing this to sink in, 'I shall be leaving next weekend, you need have no qualms on that score. I like my work, and I don't want to lose my job. But in the meantime, couldn't we suspend hostilities? For Jeremy's sake, if not for mine.'

Mrs Radley regarded her suspiciously. 'If you're so all-fire keen to get away, why don't you? Jeremy knows us now. There's nothing more for you here.'

'There's still the matter of arranging when Jeremy is to return to London,' Lesley retorted, despising the tremor in her voice as she put her thoughts into words. 'I am his mother, and I am entitled to spend some time with him during his holidays.'

'And that's the only reason why you're here?'

'What other reason could I have?'

Mrs Radley snorted. 'Maybe you've changed your mind about being independent. Maybe you've decided any meal ticket is better than none.'

Lesley shook her head defeatedly. 'You won't listen, will you, Mrs Radley? You have your own opinion, and no one can alter it.'

'I know that Carne would have been far happier marrying a girl of his own sort,' the old woman retorted, and Lesley rose abruptly to her feet.

'Like Marion Harvey, I suppose,' she suggested bitterly, and Carne's mother nodded.

'Marion would have done him proud,' she declared. 'He'd have had a capful of children by now, and not been bothering his head ov~ ~~ you've tried to turn against him.'

'That's not true!' Lesley gasped. 'I haven't tried to turn him against anyone.'

'But you will. Sending him to that boarding school! He should be brought up here, on the farm, where he belongs. And if you think a week is long enough to put him off, you're very much mistaken, by the look of it.'

Lesley turned towards the door. What use was it fighting against the future? Mrs Radley would never accept her way of thinking, any more than she could accept the older woman's. It was up to Jeremy to choose. Why hadn't she realised that before? He must decide what he wanted to do, where he wanted to live. It wasn't fair to try and manipulate him. Ultimately, it was his life and his future. Wherever he lived she knew Carne would see he got a decent education. He would want nothing less for his son and heir. And the very fact that she was talking about Carne choosing his school proved that in her mind the decision was made already.

CHAPTER EIGHT

IT was hot, really hot. Lesley could feel the sweat running in rivulets down the hollow of her spine, and even the halter-necked midi blouse she was wearing, tied in a knot beneath her breasts, and the old denims, sawn off at knee length and fraying now with long use, seemed to be clinging to her. She had tied her hair back with a black velvet ribbon, but through the course of the afternoon strands had come free, and now they chased her cheekbones as she moved, curling moistly beside her ears.

Yet for all that, she was enjoying herself, really enjoying herself for the first time in years. Haymaking was in progress, and she, along with Burt Worsley and Jeremy and two of the other men who worked for Carne, had been stacking the bundles of dried grass, forking them on to the conveyor that had been set up by the gantry in the barn. They had almost finished, and a few moments before Mary had come out of the house carrying a tray of scones and pasties, with beer for the men and iced lemonade for Lesley and Jeremy. Now they all flopped down exhaustedly, enjoying Mary's delicious baking and drinking thirstily.

Lesley, looking at Jeremy, thought how well he was looking. Gone was the faint pallor he had had from too many hours spent indoors. In its place was lightly tanned skin and healthy colour, his eyes bright and sparkling with mischief. A pang smote her as she realised she only had another day here herself. It was Saturday tomorrow, and on

Sunday Carne was driving her to York to catch the train for London.

The week had gone incredibly quickly. She could hardly believe it was a week since her arrival. She had thought the time would drag, that she would constantly be in opposition with either Carne or his mother, but it hadn't been like that.

To begin with, she had seen next to nothing of Carne. It was a hectic time of year for a farmer, and he was out and about early in the morning, rarely coming home for lunch, and disappearing into his study after dinner at night.

Jeremy was not subjected to this ostracism. He had been out with his father several times, in the Landrover or on the tractor, and once on the back of a pony Carne had apparently bought for his use. He had even been to the market at Thirsk, an outing which Lesley herself would have liked to join. Just to renew old memories, she had told herself impatiently, but it was not to be.

Mrs Radley had not drastically altered her attitude towards her daughter-in-law, but she had refrained from making too many pointed comments, and as Lesley hadn't seen a lot of her either, the days had passed without event.

For her part, Lesley had taken the opportunity to spend time outdoors. She had done quite a lot of walking, sometimes with Jeremy, sometimes not, but always accompanied by Solomon and Sheba, the two sheepdogs. They had not been at Raventhorpe when she was here before, but they soon recognised her affection for them and followed her everywhere. Even Mrs Pepperpot revised her bid for independence, and occasionally honoured Lesley by deigning to sit on her lap.

The worst day had been Wednesday when Marion Bowland had come to dinner. Mary had privately confided that she was a frequent visitor at the house, adding that in her opinion Marion was using her friendship with Mrs Radley to cement another kind of relationship with Carne. Listening to these confidences, Lesley had wondered how Mary thought *she* saw her husband. Did the other girl think that she no longer cared who her husband was friendly with, or was she trying to reassure her about an association which might easily be considered suspect? When she asked herself these questions, she had no satisfactory answers to give. Since that night at the hotel in Amblefold, she had avoided questions of that kind, and these last days had assumed the framework of a dream beyond which she did not want to think.

But Marion's presence had at least put Lesley's sojourn at the house into perspective. Her knowledge of farming matters, the way she could discuss fatstock prices with Carne, her contention that the present dry spell was becoming a liability, all demonstrated her suitability as a farmer's wife, and if she couldn't compete with Lesley's looks, she was cunning enough to use the things she did possess to full advantage.

Determining not to be left completely out of the discussion, Lesley had asked how she was managing alone at High Etherley.

'Oh,' Marion cast an amused glance at Mrs Radley, 'I'm managing very well. With Carne's help, of course.' She smiled across at him. 'Aaron left much of the actual running of the farm in my hands long before he died, and I have a very good manager.'

Lesley nodded. 'I see. But isn't it lonely up there in winter?'

'Lonely?' Marion uttered a short laugh. 'I don't have time to be lonely, Lesley. I suppose it does seem an—isolated life for someone like you,' this was said with just the right amount of sympathy, 'but I've lived here all my life, and I love it.'

Lesley glanced at her husband, seated at the end of the table. For once she caught his eyes upon her, and the brooding penetration of that scrutiny almost disarmed her. In honour of their guest, he had changed for the evening, and his dark suede pants and maroon silk shirt accentuated his swarthy tan. As he had conceded to her request that Jeremy should take his meals earlier in the evening, she had often been aware of his presence at the end of the table, but never had she encountered such dark malevolence in his gaze.

Taking her courage into both hands, she turned back to Marion and said: 'Believe it or not, but I love this area, too.'

Her statement startled words of disbelief from Mrs Radley. 'You preferred the city five years ago,' she declared. 'I don't remember you ever expressing any love for Ravensdale.'

'Perhaps I didn't love it then,' remarked Lesley carefully, not quite knowing why she was persisting with this. 'I was younger, and inexperienced. Some things mature with age——'

'You mean if I had married you now, you would have been content with our life here at Raventhorpe?' rasped Carne, breaking in on her contemptuously, and her nerve faltered.

'I—don't know, do I?' she had retorted, swallowing, and she had seen the triumphant look Marion and Mrs Radley had exchanged.

But that was two days ago now, and fortunately Marion had not offered to help them with the haymaking. In consequence, Lesley had had plenty of time to think about the things she had said, and to ponder her reasons for wanting to beat Marion at her own game. She had cleaned out the stables and groomed Carne's black hunter, Medallion; she had herded cows and chatted with the men from the Milk Marketing Board; and all the while, in the back of her mind, had been the increasingly disturbing revelation that she was enjoying renewing her interest in the farm, and that the prospect of returning to her job at West London Television had lost its charm.

She finished her lemonade now and was picking straws from the seat of her jeans when a car turned into the yard and came to a halt only a few feet from where she was standing. It was a Rolls-Royce, she saw in admiration, of vintage years, with a uniformed chauffeur behind the wheel. Only one person in the district employed a chauffeur to her knowledge, and that was Lady Alicia Skinner, the elderly daughter of the late Lord Kelbrook, who lived at Warrengill Manor. Lesley had never met her, but she had heard Mrs Radley talking about her in connection with the Women's Guild, and she knew Carne's mother was proud of the fact that she and Lady Alicia were members of the same committee. But she had not visited Raventhorpe while Lesley was living there, and her eyes were as wide and interested as Jeremy's when the old lady climbed out of the car.

Lady Alicia must have been about ten years older than Mrs Radley, but she was tall and slender and she held herself impeccably, which took years off her age. Her afternoon dress of dusty pink crêpe exactly matched the elbow-length gloves she was wearing, and her hair was long and coiled into a chignon at the nape of her neck. Her heels were as high as any Lesley had worn, and altogether she was quite an imposing figure.

Expecting her to go straight to the house, Lesley turned Jeremy firmly back to the job in hand, and was startled when an aristocratic voice enquired: 'Surely you can't be Carne's wife?'

Lesley swung about, brushing back her hair from her eyes with a grubby hand. 'I'm afraid so,' she assented apologetically. 'Would you like to see Mrs Radley?'

Lady Alicia smiled, and when she did so Lesley could see what a beautiful woman she must have been in her youth. She was still beautiful, of course, but it was the beauty of age and maturity, the blending together of colours to a gentler, more muted pattern.

'I do want to see Winifred,' she said, her eyes moving kindly to Jeremy, and Lesley thought how strange it was to hear someone call her mother-in-law by her given name. 'But when I heard you were here—with the boy—I hoped I would meet you, too.'

Lesley coloured. 'You're Lady Alicia Skinner, aren't you?' she offered awkwardly. 'I've heard about you, too, of course.'

'I thought you might.' Lady Alicia's eyes twinkled. 'And this is Jeremy.' She studied him thoughtfully for a moment. 'Yes, he's like his grandfather. He's like his father as well, naturally, but John Radley and I were friends long before young Carne came on the scene.'

Young Carne! Lesley couldn't keep the smile from her lips. Lady Alicia saw them all in a different perspective.

'I was sorry we didn't get to meet many years ago,' she continued, 'but Winifred told me you preferred not to get involved in local organisations.'

'Oh!' Lesley was taken aback for a moment. 'Did she?'

'Yes.' Lady Alicia was looking at her shrewdly. 'Such a pity. You'd have been quite an asset. It's amazing how persuasive a beautiful woman can be, even in these days. Parish councillors are men, just like any other. And we're always needing something, you know—most usually more money.'

Lesley didn't know what to say. She could hardly tell this aristocratic old lady that her mother-in-law had not even

mentioned the possibility of her joining any local organisations, and indeed had ridiculed any attempts she had made
to take an interest in parish affairs.

'I think Mrs Radley is in the drawing room,' she murmured now, unable to speak what was in her mind, but
Lady Alicia was not finished yet.

'Look here,' she said, 'I'm giving a little dinner party one
evening next week. Tuesday. How about you and your husband coming along? I never see enough of Carne, and I
know Canon Parsons and his wife would love to see you
again.'

Lesley wiped her hands down the seams of her pants and
gave a regretful shake of her head. 'I'm afraid we couldn't
do that,' she said, glancing awkwardly at Jeremy. So far she
had avoided telling him how soon she was returning to
London, and she didn't want to blurt it out now, in front
of a stranger. 'I—er—I'm sorry, but I have a previous
engagement.'

'Oh, dear.' Lady Alicia looked at her thoughtfully, and
what she was thinking was not hard to read. Obviously she
was deciding that Mrs Radley had been right in saying that
her daughter-in-law did not want to get involved in local
affairs, and probably she was regretting the impulse to offer
her a second chance.

'Jeremy, run and tell Grandma that Lady Alicia is here,'
said Lesley suddenly, unable to allow this charade to go on
any longer. And then, as he skipped towards the house, she
added hastily: 'I couldn't tell you this with Jeremy present
because he doesn't know yet, but I have to go back to
London on Sunday, so I won't be here for your dinner
party.'

'I see.' Lady Alicia nodded slowly. 'So this was just a—
visit?'

'Sort of,' agreed Lesley uncomfortably. Then: 'I'm sure you've heard that Carne and I are—well, separated.'

Lady Alicia sighed. 'I've heard that, of course. Gossip is rife in the valley, as you know. I only hoped . . .' Her voice trailed away. 'That's a fine boy you've got there. It's a pity he has to go back to London. These are his holidays, aren't they?'

'He's not going back,' said Lesley reluctantly. 'At least, not yet. He—I—Carne is—taking care of him for the holidays.'

'Oh!' Lady Alicia absorbed this consideringly, and then, looking across the yard, Lesley saw Carne's mother making her way towards them. The stick was still very much in evidence, but her face was contorted with anger as much as pain, and the look she gave her daughter-in-law was denigrating.

'You should have brought Lady Alicia into the house, Lesley!' she declared reprovingly, giving their guest an apologetic smile. 'Do come in, won't you? It won't take Mary a minute to boil the kettle.'

'As a matter of fact it's my fault,' Lady Alicia insisted, making no move to accompany her. 'I saw—Lesley, isn't it? Yes, Lesley. I saw Lesley and your grandson working here, and I stopped to have a few words with them.'

Mrs Radley's expression tightened. 'I expect she was glad of the break, Lady Alicia,' she said caustically. 'Not used to hard work, these town folks, are they?'

Lady Alicia raised her arched brows. 'I've spent a number of years living in a town, Winifred,' she told the other woman crisply, 'and I've never found urban living so soft. On the contrary, life in town can be desperately hard—and lonely. Don't you agree?'

She turned to Lesley and she was bound to answer.

'There are compensations to both,' she murmured, wishing she could be left out of the discussion, and Lady Alicia smiled rather smugly as she finally agreed to accompany her hostess back to the house.

Another black mark against me, Lesley thought wryly, as she turned to collect the tray. But the comments that Lady Alicia had made lingered as she walked slowly back to the kitchen.

She was washing her hands at the sink, when she heard the Landrover turn into the yard, and presently she could hear Jeremy's excited voice above the lower rumble of his father's. It was unusual for Carne to come back at this hour of the afternoon, Lesley thought frowningly, drying her hands. He had gone out that morning and according to Jeremy had gone to Harrogate to get a spare part for the harvester. He hadn't taken the boy with him because it was so hot, and because he said the roads would be busy with holiday traffic.

'Mum!' Jeremy came charging into the kitchen with his usual disregard for the floor. 'Mum, Daddy says he'll take me swimming. Did you bring my trunks?'

Lesley was about to answer him as Carne came in at the door, his sweat shirt unbuttoned, his arms bronzed and muscular below the short sleeves. His hair was rumpled, as if he had been running his hands through it, and he looked tired as if the day had not been a success.

'I—well, no,' she answered Jeremy now, seeing how his face drooped at her words. 'But they wouldn't have been any use to you anyway. You've grown out of them. If you want to go swimming, take an extra pair of underpants.'

'Can I? Oh, can I?' Jeremy looked from one to the other of them, and Carne made an indifferent gesture.

'If your mother has no objections.' He frowned as he

looked at his wife. 'You look hot. What have you been doing?'

'We've been haymaking,' declared Jeremy proudly, and his father's eyebrows lifted.

'Both of you?'

'Well, I'm not entirely useless!' exclaimed Lesley, stung by his tone, and he made a calming movement with his hand.

'All right. I just thought you might have developed that red face when Lady Alicia came to call.'

Lesley's hand went automatically to her burning cheeks. 'I suppose you saw the car.'

'I could hardly miss it, could I? Where's Mary? I was going to ask her to make old Kipling a cup of tea. He's sitting out there in that stuffy vehicle, dressed for all weathers! But he won't leave his post. I've asked him.'

Lesley reached for the kettle. 'I can make him a pot of tea. I expect Mary's got her hands full playing maid to your mother.'

'Yes . . .' Carne nodded, and Jeremy exclaimed: 'Well, are we going, then?'

'In a minute,' agreed Carne absently, and Lesley asked: 'Where are you taking him?'

'Just up the dam,' replied Carne briefly. Then: 'Why don't you come along? You look as though you could do with a cool swim.'

'I thought you once told me the water was too shallow to swim,' she countered, and Carne sighed.

'Marion had Aaron build up the bank about three years ago. It's made quite a difference.'

'Oh, I see. Marion,' said Lesley bitterly, and Jeremy shifted impatiently.

'Shall I go and get some more pants?' he asked, and after a moment's hesitation, Lesley nodded.

'You know where they are. In your drawer,' she said spooning tea into the pot. 'Don't pull everything out as you get them.'

Jeremy disappeared and Lesley made the tea, setting cream and sugar on a small round tray. Carne watched her for a few moments, and then he said: 'Well? Are you coming or aren't you?' and she turned to look at him.

'With Marion Bowland? No, I don't think so, thanks. I don't think I'd be very welcome.'

'I am not meeting Marion,' stated Carne grimly. 'What gave you that idea?'

Lesley's lids flickered up and then down again. 'I thought you were, that's all. After all, she's a widow now, isn't she? As eligible as she ever was.'

'What the hell are you talking about?' he snapped, and she felt her stomach muscles tightening.

'Don't pretend you don't know,' she declared, pouring the tea with hands that trembled. 'It's all past history, and you know it. We don't need to go over all that again.'

'You always had this crazy idea about me and Marion, didn't you?' he snarled. 'Just because she's been in and out of this house ever since we were children, you've resented her coming here. You've resented her familiarity, and tried to make her the excuse for your own inadequacy!'

Lesley's mouth opened, but no sound came, and Carne turned abruptly away as Mary came briskly into the kitchen. She looked surprised to find both Lesley and Carne there. but she hid her natural curiosity and left Lesley to explain why she had made the tray of tea.

'I'll carry it out to him,' said Mary at once, taking over. 'It will be quite a relief after the conversation in there.' She jerked her thumb back towards the drawing room.

Jeremy came rushing back into the kitchen at that moment, his swimming gear in his hand. Mary's eyes went straight to his feet, and shamefaced, he examined them for the dirt of the farmyard.

'They're not bad,' he muttered, an appealing look on his face, and Mary grimaced.

'Not now they're not,' she agreed. 'But I don't expect the stair carpet would agree with you.'

'I'm sorry, Mary, it was my fault,' exclaimed Lesley at once. 'I sent him upstairs. I wasn't thinking.'

Mary shook her head, her gaze moving speculatively to Carne's withdrawn features. 'I guess we all do things without thinking sometimes,' she replied reassuringly. She looked at the tray. 'Now, I'd better take this out before it gets cold.'

Jeremy looked anxiously from his mother to his father. 'What's the matter? What's wrong?'

'Nothing's wrong, darling,' said Lesley quickly. 'I—er—are you ready?'

'Are you?' enquired Carne shortly, but she shook her head.

'I don't think so. Thank you. You go along. I—well, I have some washing I want to do.'

'Oh, Mum!'

Jeremy was obviously disappointed, but his father's face was grim. 'Your mother isn't coming with us,' he said flatly. 'Does that make a difference?'

'Well . . .' Jeremy looked longingly towards the sunshine outside, and Lesley felt her patience slipping.

'Oh, go!' she cried, with an exasperated gesture. 'Just go. I'll see you—both later.'

Jeremy lingered a few moments more, but it was obvious he wanted to go swimming, and who could blame him on an afternoon like this, thought Lesley bitterly. If she was not

so stupidly thin-skinned she would go with them, but the
dam was on Bowland land, and she had no intention of
giving Marion another opportunity to cross swords with
her. Not now. Not today; when she had other things on her
mind—most particularly the things Lady Alicia had said to
her.

'Come along, then.' Carne's lips tightened as he turned
towards the door, and with a last look at his mother,
Jeremy skipped after him. And as the Landrover reversed
out of the yard, Lesley went quickly upstairs, before Mary
could come back and see the ridiculous tears in her eyes.

She was dressing for dinner that evening when Carne came
to her room.

In the week she had spent at Raventhorpe, he had never
once entered her bedroom, and the only occasion she had
seen him upstairs had been early one morning when they had
both wanted to enter the bathroom at the same time. Carne
had drawn back, indicating that she could use the bathroom
first, and when she emerged he was nowhere in sight.

Which made his present visit to her room that much more
unusual. He knocked at her door but did not wait for her
permission before entering, and she turned from applying
a tan-coloured lipstick to her mouth, overwhelmingly conscious that the satin slip she was wearing did little to conceal
her slender form. The shirt and wrap-around skirt she
planned to wear for the evening were still laid on the bed,
and she had yet to brush the silken curtain of her hair.

Carne on the other hand was fully dressed, in close-
fitting moleskin pants and a dark blue shirt, his dark hair
still glistening with drops of moisture from his shower. He
came into the room purposefully, closing the door behind
him, and leaned back against it for a few moments surveying
her through narrowed eyes.

What do you want?

The words trembled unspoken on her lips as her eyes said it for her, and he straightened and strolled lazily over to the dressing table where she was sitting. Idly, he picked up a flagon of perfume and examined its scent, and Lesley turned round again, conscious of the lipstick in her hand. But annoyingly, her fingers were no longer entirely steady, and she quickly put the lipstick down before he noticed. He was only inches away from her and the sharp flavour of his shaving lotion drifted to her nostrils, as attractive in its way as the clean male odour of his body.

When she thought her nerves would snap if he didn't speak soon, he said: 'My mother tells me that Alicia invited you and me to dinner next week.'

'Alic—oh, you mean Lady Alicia Skinner,' Lesley faltered tautly. 'Er—yes. Yes, she did. I—I explained I wouldn't be here.'

'So I hear.' Carne put down the flagon and drummed his fingers impatiently against the polished surface. 'That's a pity, don't you think? Alicia entertains only rarely.'

Lesley licked her dry lips. 'I've no doubt the invitation still stands so far as you are concerned. It's you she really wants to see.' She hesitated. 'Take Marion, why don't you? I'm sure she'd jump at the cha——'

His violent imprecation cut her off with savage abruptness, and she sought nervously for the lipstick holder again, needing something to do with her hands.

'I do not wish to take Marion to Warrengill,' he declared coldly. 'The invitation was yours—and I want you to accept it.'

Her eyes widened as she stared at his reflection in the mirror. 'Me?' she exclaimed ungrammatically. Then, with determined coolness: 'That's impossible.'

'Why is it impossible?'

'You know why. I'm leaving on Sunday.'

'You could stay over until Wednesday.'

'To go to a dinner party?' Lesley's short laugh was half hysterical. 'Oh, no, I don't think so.'

'Damn you!' Carne's hands balled into fists at his sides and he thrust them into the waistline pockets of his pants, distorting the soft moleskin. 'Oh, I realise,' he went on with heavy sarcasm, 'the kind of gatherings we enjoy can't compare to those *intellectual* parties you attend in London and that we *provincials* don't talk about the same sort of things as you *sophisticated* people——'

'That has nothing to do with it!' Lesley was on her feet now, but without shoes he had the advantage. 'You know perfectly well that I have to go back to work.'

'I also know perfectly well that you get more than one week's holiday in a year!' he retorted harshly, and she made a helpless gesture.

'I'm saving my other two weeks for when Jeremy comes back to London,' she explained and his eyes darkened grimly.

'For when Jeremy comes back to London?' he echoed. 'What do you mean?'

Lesley cleared her throat. 'You—you know,' she insisted. 'You must. At the end of the holiday . . .'

'Yes. At the end of the holiday Jeremy will be returning to school. I know, we still have that to discuss. But why should you want to save your holiday for after he returns to school?'

Lesley clenched her fists now. 'You're being deliberately obtuse. You must—you must realise that I want some time with him, too.'

'And what was your plan?' he demanded ominously.

'I—I thought you would—would allow him to return to town for the final two weeks of his holidays.'

'To be with you?'

'And—and my mother, yes.'

'Your mother doesn't want him around the place. She said so.'

'Not for the whole of the holidays, perhaps, but for two weeks . . .'

'No.' Carne shook his head, and she stared at him disbelievingly.

'What?'

'No. I said no. I won't accept it. If you want to spend time with Jeremy, come back here. I shan't stop you.'

'Carne!' Lesley's fingers curled and uncurled. 'Carne, you're being unreasonable.'

'I'm being unreasonable!' His lips twisted. 'Jeremy is far better off at the farm, running free, than confined in some stuffy flat in the city with a woman who can't stand children.' His eyes flicked scornfully over her. 'Be honest for once. Admit that he's happy here.'

Lesley held up her head. 'Oh, yes,' she said carefully, 'I know he's happy now. But I'm still here, aren't I? And he doesn't know yet that I'm leaving in two days. I don't think it would be entirely untrue to say that he's going to miss me.'

'Then don't go,' said Carne, hard-eyed. 'Stay until the end of the holidays.'

Lesley's face filled with colour. 'Stay?' she echoed faintly. 'You—you can't be serious. Why—your mother——'

'I own this farm, not my mother,' he declared coldly. Then he took a step towards her. 'Why not stay?' He looked down at where the hollow between her breasts was visible above the low-cut neckline of the slip. 'I haven't asked you to leave.'

Lesley's breathing felt constricted. 'Are—are you asking

me to—to come back to you?' she got out huskily, but Carne merely shook his head.

'I wouldn't do that,' he said, and she was shocked at the way his words dismayed her. 'All I'm suggesting is that you spend a couple of months at the farm. Mary says you're far too thin, and I agree with her.'

Lesley drew an unsteady breath. 'It—it's out of the question.' She almost choked on the words and his expression changed from wary interrogation to grim impatience. 'I—there's still my job.'

'To hell with your job!' he snapped, raking back his hair with an angry hand. 'That means more to you than anything, doesn't it?'

'No——'

'Don't give me that. You're one of those females who needs to prove themselves in a man's world! Who hasn't the sense to see that there's more to being a woman than competing on a man's terms.'

'I wouldn't expect you to see it any other way!' she retorted hotly, stung as always by his determined opposition to women's equality. 'But let me tell you those chauvinist attitudes are out of date in today's world. The men I associate with judge a woman on her ability, not her sex!'

'Oh, I believe it.' His lips curled. 'The—men you associate with would! But then they've conceded so much ground already, they don't have much choice, do they?'

'What do you mean? They're decent people, just like——'

'Are they?'

'—like any civilised——'

'Oh, civilised, is it? Well, I'm bloody sick of hearing that word. Civilised! Particularly as every time you use it, you seem to imply that I'm not!'

'And are you?' she taunted recklessly. 'Would you call

this conversation civilised? Would you call what you're doing to me civilised?'

'What I'm doing to you!' He stared at her incredulously, his eyes darkening with kindling anger. 'My God, what am I doing to you? What *should* I be doing to you? Maybe that's a more relevant question. You're my wife. There's a wholly—civilised way of settling this argument!'

'No, Carne . . .'

'No, Carne!' he mimicked her, but when she backed away from him, he came after her so that when her legs encountered the side of the bed, she had no alternative but to sink down on to it.

'Will you please get out of my room?' she demanded, forcing the note of hysteria out of her voice, but the rise and fall of her breasts seemed to fascinate Carne and he squatted down before her, his hands sliding possessively along her thighs to her hips.

'I don't see why I should,' he said thickly, bending his head to kiss her hands lying palm-upwards in her lap, and her fingers closed convulsively. 'Such soft skin,' he added, his lips straying up over her arm to her shoulder, pushing the strap of her slip aside to expose one pointed breast.

'Carne . . .' she protested again, as he levered himself on to the bed beside her, but almost of their own volition, her hands were probing inside his shirt, and when his mouth found hers, her lips parted to the pressure of his.

His kiss was hard and passionate, compelling her back against the slippery quilt, its softness cool against her bare back. His fingers had disposed of the other strap of her slip, and his hands found the burgeoning fullness of her breasts, crushed beneath the hair-coarsened muscles of his chest. His shirt was unbuttoned and her palms slid across his back, warm against the dampness of his spine.

'Carne,' she breathed, when his mouth released hers to seek the creamy curve of her breast. 'Carne, it's time we were going down for dinner . . .' but her words had little effect.

'I'm not hungry,' he replied huskily, blazing a trail of kisses across her midriff and down to the hollow of her navel. 'Not for food anyway. Hmm, you smell warm and womanly. Don't talk about going downstairs . . . not yet anyway . . .'

'Carne, your mother's going to wonder where we are,' she persisted, as he spread his length upon her, but her body was already yielding to the thrusting demand of his.

'Stop worrying about other people,' he groaned, grasping one of her hands and pressing his lips to her palm. 'Don't pretend you really care . . .'

'I do, I do,' she insisted, but the look in his eyes drove all the breath out of her. 'No, Carne,' she said again weakly, as his hand sought the buckle of his belt, but it was a token resistance and he knew it.

'Help me,' he said hoarsely, and her fingers went automatically to the buckle as a strangled cry arrested them.

'My God, Carne!' Mrs Radley choked from the doorway. 'What in heaven's name do you think you're doing?'

Carne lifted his head and looked across at his mother with deadly inplacability. Lesley, shifting in hot embarrassment beneath him, thought she would die if he ever looked at her like that, and his mother was well aware of the cold fury in his eyes.

'Get out of here, Mother!' he told her harshly. 'Get out and stay out!'

Mrs Radley swayed at the force of his rejection but she stood her ground. 'And—and what shall I tell this man on the telephone?' she asked tremulously. 'What shall I say to him?'

'What man?'

Lesley could feel the force of Carne's anger rippling through him. Humiliation, and the imprisonment of his weight, kept her where she was, but she dreaded what his mother must be thinking of her.

'A Mr Petrie,' Mrs Radley pronounced with evident satisfaction. 'A Mr Lance Petrie. He says—*she* works for him.'

'Lance?'

Lesley's involuntary echo of the name seemed to cleave a wedge between them, and with a muffled oath Carne swung his legs over the side of the bed and got abruptly to his feet.

'Petrie, did you say?' he demanded of his mother, and at her nod, he looked again at his wife.

Lesley was trying, not very successfully, to wriggle her slip back up over her shoulders and seeing the struggle she was having, Carne uttered another curse and jerked her upright, pulling up the straps himself and securing them in place.

'There!' he said contemptuously. 'Now you can go and speak to your employer. Tell him he didn't interrupt anything very important.'

'Carne . . .' Lesley slid her legs off the bed and looked up at him helplessly, but he turned away. 'I—well, where shall I take the call?'

'In the study, where else?' declared Carne coldly, fastening the buttons of his shirt. 'Put your clothes on first, will you? I'd prefer it if the men I employ don't get the chance to see my *wife* half naked!'

Then he turned to his mother, her eyes wide with indignation as she still hovered in the doorway. 'You can go,' he said. 'I shan't touch her again. But next time you enter a room, try knocking first.'

'You should thank me,' Mrs Radley burst out, refusing to

let him have the last word. 'I've probably prevented you from doing something you'd bitterly regret!'

Carne's mouth twisted. 'Probably,' he agreed, as Lesley pushed her arms into the sleeves of her shirt. 'And don't misjudge the situation, will you? Lesley would be the first to concede that your arrival was a welcome escape!'

CHAPTER NINE

THE plane was half an hour late landing at Heathrow, and Lesley's already strained nerves had stretched ominously. Surely it wasn't too much to expect that the fifty-minute flight from Paris should have been on time, but a lightning strike at the airport had delayed outgoing flights and brought all baggage handling to a standstill. Still, it had been no hardship for Lesley to carry her overnight bag. Only the unwarranted delay had added to her persistent state of tension. Lance was expecting her back in the office by four o'clock at the latest, but now she would be lucky to be there by five, bearing in mind the steadily increasing traffic flow towards the peak periods.

She was lucky enough to get a taxi almost straight away although as they joined the stream of cars making for the city she wondered whether it wouldn't have been quicker to take the underground. Still, she thought wearily, at least the air was cooler above ground and she was not to suffer the discomfort of being crammed into a metal tube with a crowd of others like so many sardines.

Staring through the taxi windows, however, she could not help but compare her surroundings with the peace and tranquillity of Raventhorpe. She had done that frequently since she came back to town, and she had determinedly put it down to the fact that she needed a holiday. Those few days in the country had been far too brief, and she thought longingly of the two further weeks she was permitted at the end of August. She would get away then, she thought, leave the city altogether; but whether or not she would return to Yorkshire was very much in the balance.

Leaving Jeremy had not been the traumatic experience she had anticipated. Lance's phone call had had more than one reaction. His request that she should return to town a day earlier than planned had given her a reason for leaving, and Jeremy had accepted without question the suggestion that he should stay on at the farm. Indeed, she remembered with bitterness, he had obviously been relieved when she offered him the opportunity, albeit nominally, and when his father had driven her to York to catch the train to London, he had waved her off without tears. Maybe they would come later, she reflected, at bedtime perhaps, or the next time he fell and injured himself. But she would not wish them on him even though it hurt to feel herself unwanted.

After that scene in the bedroom, Carne had ignored her and as his mother blamed her for what had happened, the atmosphere in the house had not been friendly. But Mrs Radley did not risk her son's displeasure again by voicing her opinion on the matter, and it was left to Mary to offer the girl her good wishes.

'Will you be coming back?' she asked, when Lesley went to say goodbye to her, but Lesley couldn't answer her.

'You'll let me know if—if Jeremy's unhappy, won't you?' she appealed, voicing the fears that haunted her, and Mary nodded.

'Of course. But then Mr Carne'll do that, don't you fret,' she replied reassuringly. 'And holidays don't last for ever.'

'I know.' Lesley wished this knowledge set her mind at rest. But it didn't. There might be a whole new set of problems at the end of the holidays.

The taxi lurched across the over-pass and she fanned herself with the newspaper she had bought in Paris. She had

read it from cover to cover in the departure lounge at
Charles de Gaulle airport, but she had tucked it into the
strap of her briefcase when she boarded the plane and it
was still with her. Lance might enjoy reading about the
present political unrest in France, she decided. He was fana-
tically interested in the struggle for power. No doubt that
was why he found her association with Carne so interesting.

She caught her lower lip between her teeth and bit hard.
Ahead of them in the stream of traffic was a Citroën estate
car similar to the one Carne drove, only cleaner. There were
three people in the car, a man, a woman and a child, and
the significance of their relationship smote her painfully. It
could so easily have been herself and Carne and Jeremy
instead of which she had opted for a precarious freedom.

Precarious! Precarious indeed, when she considered how
nearly she had come to betraying herself. Who would have
believed that after all these years Carne had only to touch
her for her to respond to him like any impressionable schoolgirl? Who would have believed that age and experience
could count for so little when confronted with the most basic
demands of the flesh? It seemed strange when in those
months after Jeremy had been born their relationship had
practically ceased to exist, and Carne had turned away from
her to seek his pleasures elsewhere. How could that situation have changed? Unless . . . unless it was *she* who had
changed . . .

But she hadn't, she told herself severely, her fingers
drumming nervously against her briefcase. She was allowing her anxiety for Jeremy to colour her reactions to his
father, letting a physical reaction effect a physical change
and deluding herself that it was anything more than that.
And yet nothing could alter the fact that when something
had happened to exclude conclusively the possibility of her

being pregnant she had cried herself to sleep . . .

Lance was in a black mood when she got to the studios, and her tentative account that the European link for his programme about nuclear reactors had been arranged met with only the briefest of approvals.

'Where the devil have you been?' he demanded, as soon as she had delivered her report. 'I expected you back over an hour ago, and that situation has not been improved by your mother ringing me every five minutes to find out where you are.'

'*Mother?*' Lesley stared at him in dismay. 'Mother's been ringing here?'

'Yes. Yes. Haven't I just said so?' Lance was not in the mood to be tolerant. 'Anyway, now that you are here, you can start on that report of Simon's. About the by-elec——'

'But what did she want?' Lesley was still getting over the shock of her mother ringing the studios. She had never done that before, and visions of her having had a heart attack and being unable to reach help kept rushing through her head.

Lance sighed. 'How the hell do I know?' he exclaimed, spreading his hands in a gesture of impatience. 'I didn't ask her. She tried to ring you yesterday, too, but I told her you weren't due back from Paris till today.'

'But she knows that,' protested Lesley anxiously. 'Oh, she wouldn't have rung unless it was important? Why didn't you let me know?'

'In Paris?' Lance looked scandalised. 'Look, Lesley, if your mother can't manage alone for two nights, it's a bloody bad job!'

Lesley pressed her lips together. 'Well, I'll have to ring her now. Before I start anything else.'

Lance contained his anger with evident difficulty. 'Very

well,' he said. 'Ring her. But I expect that report about the by-election on my desk first thing tomorrow morning.'

'Yes, *sir*!' declared Lesley, with cold politeness, and Lance slammed back into his office.

The telephone seemed to ring for a long time before Mrs Matthews answered it, and when she did she sounded almost put out. 'Lesley!' she cried. 'Oh, you would ring right in the middle of the serial, wouldn't you? You know I've watched it right from the beginning, and today is the last episode.'

The sound Lesley made was strangled, but she managed not to sound too angry as she said: 'Mother, it is only a children's serial, and may I remind you, you have been trying to get me for the past twenty-four hours?'

'Oh, I know.' Mrs Matthews sighed, evidently giving up all hope of seeing the completion of the play. 'Well, as a matter of fact, it wasn't that important . . .'.

'What wasn't important?' Lesley's voice was taut. 'Mother have you been ill? Has your heart——'

'No, no.' Mrs Matthews sounded almost amused. 'It wasn't anything to do with me. It was just a phone call I had from Raventhorpe——'

'*Raventhorpe?*' Lesley's mouth went dry. 'What about? Is it Jeremy? Has something happened? Has he had an accident?'

'Calm yourself!' Mrs Matthews clicked her tongue. 'I'm trying to tell you. Jeremy, it seems, has got measles——'

'Measles!'

'—and so, unfortunately, has Mrs Radley.'

'Carne's mother?'

'Apparently.' Mrs Matthews sighed. 'I had this call from someone called Mary, is that right?'

'Mary?' Lesley nodded 'Mary Walker, yes.' She felt her

nails digging into her palms. 'So what did she suggest?'

'Suggest?' Mrs Matthews sounded surprised. 'She didn't suggest anything. She just said that you'd probably want to know.'

'Oh, I do. I do.' Lesley was already thinking ahead. If Jeremy had measles and his grandmother had measles, Mary was going to have her hands full. And Carne . . .

'Is that all, dear?' Her mother was obviously agitating to get back to the television, and Lesley had to let her go. But when she had replaced the receiver after promising that she would be home in time for supper, she sat staring at the inanimate object with troubled eyes.

How would Carne cope with two invalids on his hands? Mary could handle so much, but with Mrs Radley incapacitated there was bound to be a lot of running up and down stairs to do. As for Jeremy, he would not be at all happy, and her heart ached for him. If he had it badly, he would be terribly distressed, and how could Mary devote enough time to him when she had other chores to attend to?

There was nothing else for it. She would have to ask Lance if she could take her other two weeks' holiday immediately, instead of at the end of the month. If Carne objected to her arrival, it was just too bad. She could keep out of his way, and maybe she could prove to him, and herself, that she was not the useless ornament Mrs Radley had always thought her.

Lance, however, was not disposed to be generous.

'Do you realise you've already taken ten days at a time that was convenient for you, but not for me, and now you expect me to turn round and say yes, go along, take as much time as you like, when the studios are already understaffed due to holidays, and I'm having to work every hour God sends to keep up to date with the situation.'

'But Lance, this is an emergency . . .'

'How is it? So the kid's got measles. What of it? Lots of kids get measles. It's not the end of the world. His father will cope——'

'I don't know that he will.'

'It's not as if it was Carne who was begging you to help him out. It's some girl who works for him, who's probably scared to death she's going to have to work a little harder because of it.'

'That's not true!' Lesley's face was pink. 'Mary's not like that.'

Lance took a deep breath, and shuffled the papers on his desk. 'Well, Lesley,' he said, and the very quietness of his tone was ominous, 'let me put it this way: eight years ago, when you took it into your head to walk out on me and all I'd done for you, I gave in gracefully. When your marriage didn't work out and you came running back, I gave in again. But this time I'm damn sure you're not going to make a fool out of me!'

Lesley sighed. All he had said was true, but surely as a man who studied people for a living he must know that circumstances altered cases. Her behaviour had been not so much irresponsible as ill-advised, and she had paid for it in so many ways.

'You won't try and understand, will you?' she exclaimed. 'Of course I'm worried about Jeremy, who wouldn't be? But it's not just that. If Mrs Radley is ill as well——'

'Lesley, you never learn, do you?' Lance sounded frustrated. 'You said yourself when you got back that Carne's mother still hated the sight of you. Now you're trying to tell me that you want to go back there to look after her!' He shook his head. 'You're crazy!'

Lesley held up her head. 'Why do you think I want to go

back, then?' she demanded, and Lance's mouth curved down.

'For the same reason you went to Ravensdale in the first place,' he retorted laconically. 'Because you're infatuated with that hunk of skin and muscle you call a husband!'

'Infatuated!' Lesley's face burned now. 'I think you're the crazy one, Lance.'

'Do you?' He shrugged. 'You're entitled to your opinion of course. But then I'm entitled to mine, too, aren't I?'

'Why would I walk out on Carne if I was infatuated with him!' she protested.

'God knows, I don't.'

'And in any case, infatuation is a—a fleeting thing. It wouldn't last—eight years!'

'That's your problem, not mine.' Lance tipped his chair on to its back legs. 'Well, you've heard my ultimatum. What's yours?'

'Ultimatum?' She felt confused. 'I don't have an ultimatum.'

'You do. You have to decide. Carne Radley—or W.L.T.V.'

Lesley stared at him. 'That's—that's blackmail!'

'Hardly blackmail,' retorted Lance dryly. 'If you leave, I've got nothing to gain by it.'

Lesley sniffed and he handed her a tissue from the box on his desk without speaking. She blew her nose, and then resumed her consideration of his unyielding features.

'Just give me a few days,' she begged. 'It's Friday tomorrow. Give me until next Tuesday or Wednesday, just to assure myself that—that Jeremy's all right.'

Lance's mouth tightened. 'Why should I?'

'Compassion?' she suggested with an attempt at facetiousness that didn't quite come off.

'Three days, eh?' Lance seemed to be considering it as

he reached for a cigar from the box on his desk. 'All right,' he said at last. 'Three days, and three days only. If you're not back here Wednesday morning, you're out of a job, right?'

'Oh, thank you.' Lesley could have hugged him, and she tackled the report she had to type with renewed confidence. If she left first thing in the morning, she could be there by lunchtime, which would give her three whole days before she had to start back.

Her mother reacted in much the same way as Lance had done.

'Why on earth should it matter to you if Mrs Radley is ill?' she exclaimed. 'She won't want your help.'

'No, but Jeremy might,' replied Lesley, folding pants into her suitcase. 'Besides, I want to see Jeremy for myself. Measles can cause complications, and I want to be sure he's properly looked after.'

Mrs Matthews sounded disgusted. 'All this talk about independence,' she snorted. 'I really thought you might enjoy being free of the responsibility for Jeremy, but you're not, are you? Your idea of freedom seems to encompass a great deal of commitment.'

'I am his mother,' said Lesley quietly, considering the contents of her wardrobe, and Mrs Matthews shook her head.

'I sometimes wonder why you pretend to want to live alone,' she declared spitefully. 'It seems to me that if you'd had a little more guts you might still be mistress of Raventhorpe!'

'Guts had nothing to do with it!' retorted Lesley, stung into retaliation, but clearly her mother did not believe her.

'Guts—and staying power,' she repeated, going out the door. 'And the ability to stand up and fight for what's yours, instead of running away like a frightened rabbit!'

Lesley couldn't help remembering what her mother had said on the long drive up to Yorkshire. It was true from the distance of time and experience, her reasons for walking out lacked conviction. But at the time they had been convincing enough, and just because the years had glossed over the crueller aspects of Carne's behaviour, nothing could alter the fact that he had shown little sympathy for her exigencies.

Perhaps her youth was the key, after all. Perhaps she had been too defensive, too ready to take offence over small digressions. Mrs Radley would not have been able to hurt her if she had been more sure of herself, of Carne, and of her position in the household. As it was, she had allowed every setback to become a defeat, every difference of opinion to escalate into an all-out row.

Before Jeremy was born, she had had more self-confidence, but the strains of her pregnancy combined with her weakness afterwards had made everything so much more intense. She had been taut and nervous, defensive of her role as Jeremy's mother, frightened and uncertain when Carne seemed to be turning away from her.

That her fears had been magnified by Mrs Radley's attitude she could see now, but she might have swum through the treacherous waters if it had not been for Marion Bowland.

Marion Harvey, as she had been then. Lesley swung out to overtake a furniture wagon, her fingers tightening on the wheel. Without her intervention, things might have been so different. But Marion was an embittered girl herself. She had not visited Raventhorpe as frequently as she did just to see Mrs Radley. On Carne's own admission, they had been friends since childhood, and she had treated the

house as a second home. Lesley tried to put herself in
Marion's position, but it wasn't easy. She couldn't see herself coming to the farm so frequently once Carne was
married and presumably lost to her, she couldn't see herself ignoring the signs and behaving as if this was just a
temporary setback, she couldn't see herself insinuating her
opinion into Carne's ear and displaying in so many ways
how much more fitted to be his wife she was.

And yet Marion had done all these things. From the first,
she had treated Lesley as a rather immature infatuation on
Carne's part, never taking her opinion seriously, constantly
seeking ways to make her look small. Aided and abetted
by Carne's mother, Marion had ridiculed her rival on every
possible occasion, and when Lesley returned home after
having had the baby, Marion had become an integral part
of their lives.

Lesley couldn't accept it. She didn't want to accept it.
She didn't want Marion around her, pretending to help her,
handling the baby. And what should have been a bond
forged between her and Carne became a wedge to drive
them apart. Because of Marion, and Carne's total refusal to
ask her to keep away, Lesley directed all the pent-up love
inside her towards the child, and in so doing drove Carne
to do what Marion had wanted all along—take his pleasures
elsewhere. Lesley didn't need to be told what was going on.
Carne moving his belongings out of her room was enough,
and Mrs Radley's smug condemnation had been more than
she could bear.

It was ominously cloudy when she reached the turn-off
for Ravensdale, and driving up through the valley spots of
rain splattered the windscreen. But despite the over-
hanging gloom, she was exhilarated, a feeling she had never
associated with Raventhorpe before. It was like going home,

and her heart beat a little faster as she bumped across the cattle grid and drove towards the house.

A glance at her watch told her it was after one o'clock, which meant that lunch was probably over. Still, she could always make herself a sandwich, she thought, as a low rumble of protest came from her stomach. She left the Mini at the side of the house and walked round to the kitchen door. She was surprised Mary hadn't come out to see who it was, but then she probably had her hands full.

Her first impression as she came through the kitchen door was dismay, followed almost immediately by amazement. Mary's kitchen had never looked like this. There was a pile of unwashed dishes in the sink, the table was spread with the remains of several meals by the look of it, and the floor was grimed with dirt from the farmyard. But the most amazing thing of all was that it was not Mary who was standing by the draining board, peeling potatoes, but Marion Bowland.

Suppressing the instinctive urge to turn her back on it all, Lesley stepped reluctantly through the door, and as if aware of the darkening shadow she cast, Marion looked round. If Lesley had been surprised to see Marion, it was not more so than Marion was surprised to see her, and an expression of angry resentment spread over her plain face.

'What are you doing here?' she demanded aggressively, and Lesley, rallying her forces, composed her features.

'I could ask you the same,' she countered pleasantly. 'Where's Mary?'

'Mary!' Marion made the word sound like an insult. 'Mary's not here any more.'

'Not here?' Lesley was taken aback, although she ought to have guessed something of the kind when she saw the state of the kitchen. 'You mean, she's ill, too?'

'No, I don't mean that,' retorted Marion short. 'I mean she's not here. She left. Walked out—just like you did.'

Lesley let that go, but her mind was racing furiously. When had Mary walked out? And why? Was that before she telephoned Lesley or after? But most importantly now, who was taking care of Jeremy?

'How is—my son? And Mrs Radley, of course?' she asked, walking further into the room. 'I—understand they've been ill.'

Marion's mouth tightened. 'Now who would tell you a thing like that?' she snapped. 'Not Carne, I'll be bound. He's got enough on his hands without inviting another useless individual to Raventhorpe.'

Lesley itched to respond in kind, particularly in the circumstances, but she let a mocking appraisal of the rooms' deficiencies suffice and said instead: 'Never mind how I know. I do. Where are they? Where's Jeremy?'

'In his room, I expect,' said Marion sharply. 'Have you come to take him back with you? I hope so. Miserable little devil, crying all the time!'

'Crying . . .' Lesley's hands trembled, but Marion was going on.

'Yes. Wants attention every minute of the day, he does. A proper baby. Just because I slapped him when he wet the bed, he won't have anything to do with me. As if I haven't got enough on my hands——'

But she was talking to herself. Lesley had opened the door into the hall and was already hurrying up the stairs, trying to quell the almost violent fury she had felt when Marion said she had slapped him for something of which he would be bitterly ashamed anyway.

She burst into Jeremy's room to find him sprawled on the floor, playing with the soldier dolls Carne had provided for his use, but when the door opened he sprang to his feet, to stand facing the intruder in evident defiance. Then he realised it was not Marion but his mother who stood in the doorway, and with a disbelieving little cry, he flung himself into her arms.

Some minutes later Lesley disentangled herself from his clinging fingers and drew him down on to the bed beside her. He looked pathetically thin in pyjamas that seemed a size too big for him, but thankfully his spots were subsiding and no longer so irritable.

'Now,' she said, having listened to his chapter of accidents told between hiccoughing sobs, 'do you know why Mary's not here?'

Jeremy sniffed a few times, blew his nose, and then nodded. 'I think so.'

'Go on, then—why?'

'It was 'cos of me, I s'pose.'

'Why because of you?'

Jeremy hesitated. 'When—when I had an accident—you know,' he gestured to the bed behind them. 'Well, then Mary got angry with Mrs Bowland because—because she smacked me.'

'I see.' Lesley frowned, silently applauding Mary's action. 'But that really doesn't explain why Mary left.'

Jeremy frowned. 'I—I think Mrs Bowland complained to Daddy, and he spoke to Mary.'

'Oh!' The position was becoming clearer, although how Carne could have taken Marion's side, she didn't know. And yet wasn't that what he had always done? She shook her head. She was jumping to conclusions again, but somehow she couldn't help it.

'I'm glad you've come back,' declared Jeremy fervently, edging closer. 'I have missed you.'

'Have you, darling?' Lesley felt a moment's scepticism. Until his illness, Jeremy seemed to have managed very well —as Carne had said he would. Now she said: 'What about Grandma? How is she?' deliberately hiding her own feelings of emptiness.

Jeremy looked thoughtful. 'She's all right, I think,' he said doubtfully. 'She spends most of the time in bed. I haven't seen her much, only with Daddy.'

'I wonder when Mary left,' murmured Lesley, returning to the most unpalatable subject of all, and Jeremy frowned.

'I think it was two—maybe three days ago,' he said. 'Mrs Bowland said I had to stay in bed, 'cos I was poorly, and she brought up my meals. Mary used to come up and see me, though, and then she just stopped coming. I asked Mrs Bowland where she was and she said she'd left.'

'I see.' The whole picture was falling into place like the pieces of a jigsaw. 'Well, I suppose I ought to go and see Grandma.'

'Not now,' said Jeremy at once, and when his mother looked questioningly at him, he added: 'She's asleep. When Mrs Bowland brought my lunch she said I wasn't to make any noise 'cos Grandma was going to have a nap.'

'Oh!' Lesley digested this, and then she rose to her feet, going across to the window and looking out thoughtfully for a moment. She could see a tractor moving in the distance, weaving brown furrows against the burned earth, wavering through the streaks of rain that had threatened earlier. Her mind was busy with the reasons why Mary had chosen to telephone her, and only the hollow emptiness inside her brought her thoughts back to the present.

Turning to Jeremy, she ran a light hand over his forehead, finding to her relief that his temperature seemed normal. Obviously, he was over the worst of the disease, but probably Marion was right in confining him to his room. His tray with its congealing mess of scrambled eggs and bacon attracted her attention, and picking it up, she said:

'I'm going downstairs now to make myself a sandwich. You get back into bed like a good boy and I'll fetch you some milk and biscuits up later.'

'Will you?' Jeremy was endearingly eager. 'I couldn't eat that!' He indicated the tray. 'I hate fatty bacon.'

'Yes, well . . .' Lesley was loath to be too sympathetic. 'You be a good boy, and I'll be back in a little while.'

On the landing, she looked at the door to Mrs Radley's room and then turned determinedly away. If Mrs Radley was sleeping, she would not risk disturbing her. Time enough to suffer her complaints when there was no alternative.

When she reached the kitchen she found Marion had made herself a pot of tea, and was presently seated at the untidy table, drinking it. One of Mary's homemade spice cakes had been set on a plate, and Marion had cut off a hefty wedge and was presently ploughing her way through it.

Lesley carried Jeremy's tray to the drainer and lifting his plate, scraped its contents into the waste bin. Marion watched her with brooding eyes, and then she said sourly: 'Well? Has he told you all his troubles?'

Lesley ignored this and after a quick look round, went towards the larder. The stone-floored larder was as big as her mother's kitchen at the flat, and its shelves were usually filled with Mary's pie and puddings. Today, however, only half a side of ham sat unappetisingly on a plate, and even the bread in the bread-bin was stale and hard.

However, it would have to do, and Lesley carried the bread and the cutting board into the kitchen and carved herself a slice of ham to make a sandwich.

Marion viewed her activity with scarcely concealed resentment, but Lesley refused to be intimidated. She had as much right here as Marion Bowland, she told herself, although she doubted whether Marion or Carne would agree with her.

With a sandwich inside her, she felt more ready to face what was to come, and avoiding Marion's dour indignation, she poured herself a cup of tea from the pot and drank it while she put the bread and ham away again. Then, still ignoring the other girl, she went to the sink and began running water into the basin.

That made Marion sit up. 'What're you doing?'

'Washing up,' declared Lesley quietly. 'It looks as though someone should.'

Marion pushed back her chair and got to her feet. 'There's no need for you to soil your hands. I can manage.'

'I doubt it,' retorted Lesley, squeezing washing fluid into the water which fortunately was hot. 'Besides, I'm quite willing to do my share.'

'Your share!' Marion stared at her scornfully. 'What do you know about running a house?'

'As much as you, by the look of things,' retorted Lesley quickly, and Marion flushed.

'If you had those two on your hands all day long——' she was beginning, jerking her thumb towards the upstairs rooms, when the sound of a thud followed almost immediately by shrill sobbing came from that direction.

Shaking the water from her hands, Lesley sped across the room and up the stairs again. The sobbing was coming from Jeremy's room, and she rushed in, expecting the worst. He was sitting on the floor at the bottom of the bed, crying and holding his head, and when she hurried to him he buried his face against her.

'What is it?' she exclaimed, feeling the thudding of her

heart against her ribs, and Jeremy sobbed out his sorry tale.

'I—I fell,' he cried, sniffing miserably. 'I fell off the end of the bed.'

Lesley's eyes looked over his head to the square rail at the end of his bed. With brows drawn together, she echoed: 'You fell off the end of the bed?'

'Yes.' Jeremy turned injured eyes up to her. 'I hurt my head.'

'But how could you fall off the end of the bed?' exclaimed Lesley, incredulously. 'The rail would stop you. And what were you doing at the end of the bed anyway?'

Jeremy's mouth trembled. 'You'll be cross with me.'

'Why will I be cross with you?'

He hesitated. 'Because I fell.'

A faint line of irritation was etching its way across Lesley's forehead. 'Jeremy, how did you fall?'

'I just fell.'

'Jeremy!'

'Oh, well, I—I was playing pirates, and—I was sword-fighting and—and——'

'—and you climbed on to the end of the bed?'

Jeremy nodded.

'You know that was very naughty, don't you?' Lesley stood up, bringing him to his feet as she did so. 'I asked you to get into bed until I came back, didn't I?'

'I'm sick of being in bed,' complained Jeremy sulkily, and Lesley sighed.

'I know you are, but that's the way it has to be.'

'Why can't I come downstairs with you?'

'Because I have work to do in the kitchen, and the door's open, and I can't have you catching a chill.'

'Why can't Mrs Bowland do the work?'

'Because she can't.' Lesley tried not to sound too impatient, but reaction from Mary's absence, Marion's hostility, and Jeremy's lack of understanding was beginning to set in. 'Now, get into bed. Here's the soldier dolls you were playing with before. You look after them until I have time to come back and talk to you.'

Jeremy was not happy, but he took the dolls without complaint and Lesley made her way back downstairs. Marion had not tackled the dishes in her absence as she had thought she might, but had poured herself another cup of tea which she raised mockingly in Lesley's direction when she reappeared.

'Is the little darling making a nuisance of himself?' she enquired silkily, and Lesley had to bite her tongue to stop herself from being blisteringly rude.

There seemed no end to the pile of dishes that mounted on the draining board. Breakfast dishes, dinner dishes; dishes whose hardened contents bore witness to the fact that they had been there more than a few hours. Lesley's arms ached by the time she had scoured all the pans clean, and then she had to set about drying them.

Although the fine drizzle had cooled the air a little, it was still excessively humid, and she was sweating profusely by the time Jeremy shouted down the stairs. Aware of Marion's silent derision, she climbed the stairs again, only to find her son wanted her assistance to find one of his toy cannon balls which had gone missing.

'Jeremy!' There was a definite edge to his mother's voice now. 'I can't waste time looking for toy cannon balls. You'll have to find it yourself. And don't shout down the stairs again. You know Grandma is supposed to be resting.'

Jeremy's jaw began to wobble. 'You're not going to be cross with me, too, are you?' he mumbled. 'I only wanted you to help me.'

Lesley controlled her temper with difficulty. 'No, of course I'm not going to be cross with you,' she exclaimed. 'But try and entertain yourself for a while, Jeremy. I promise I'll come back as quickly as I can.'

Downstairs again, she found her legs were actually a little shaky themselves, due no doubt to the unaccustomed journeys up and down the stairs. At the flat there were no stairs, and even at work, there were lifts to take one from floor to floor.

'You look worn out already,' remarked Marion callously. She had returned to peeling potatoes and her cup, saucer and plate were now waiting to be washed.

Her sarcasm was the last straw. Lesley's control snapped. 'Well, at least I'll improve with time!' she countered grimly, and Marion's face blazed with colour.

'How—how dare you—sp-speak to me like that?' she choked indignantly, but Lesley stood her ground.

'I'll speak to you how I like,' she declared coldly. 'For someone with such an incredibly thick hide you have a remarkably thin skin.'

'Why, you—you listen to me——'

'No, you listen to me, Marion. I've been very patient, too patient, I see that now, but years ago I was young and immature, and too insecure to fight you at your own game. But things are different now and I've had it up to here with your unsubtle barbs and innuendoes. You think you're so efficient, don't you? Just because you can milk a cow and estimate how much grain you'll need to see you through the winter! Well, let me tell you, there's more to living with a man than you'll have learned from Aaron Bowland who was old enough to be your grandfather! Why you can't even take care of one small boy, and you think you make me look small! You're wrong. And what's more, you're wrong about

Carne, too. He still *wants* me, do you know that? He can't keep his hands off me!'

'That's not true!' Marion was pale now, but Lesley was unrepentant.

'It is true. It is. I can prove it. Did you know he arranged for us to spend a night at an hotel before coming here?'

'That means nothing!' Marion's lips twisted. 'That's not proof! Even if you did spend the night at an hotel, which I doubt, why should I believe anything you say when Carne's already told me that there's no question of a reconciliation?'

Lesley's stomach plunged sickeningly. Had Carne discussed their affairs with Marion, then? Had he confided in her? Had he already discussed the possibility of the divorce his mother had told her about? And why did it matter to her anyway, when she would be returning to London in three days?

But it did matter and she knew it. And what was more, Marion knew it. Already her lips were curving upward in a smile of triumph as she guessed she had struck the right note.

'Poor Lesley,' she said, but there was no sympathy in her voice. 'Do you think I don't know how you feel? I knew all along what drove you to walk out on Carne. All that talk of independence, when what you really meant was inadequacy. Carne was never happy with you, you could never satisfy him, a skinny little townie, whose only ability was to get pregnant and force him to marry you!'

'You're lying!' Now Lesley was on the defensive, but she couldn't help it.

'I'm not lying. That child was born less than nine months after Carne put his ring on your finger. Do you think I'm stupid? Do you think the people of the dale are stupid? We knew. We all knew why he had to marry you!'

Lesley gasped, but she knew it would do no good to argue. And besides, why should she? Why should she justify herself to a woman who had hated and despised her from the very beginning? But Marion's contemptuous words did have another effect, they inspired the glimmer of an idea inside her, an idea which although quite outrageous would spike her guns once and for all.

Breaking in on the other girl's tirade about so-called intellectuals, and what did they know about farming, she said:

'You are right about one thing, Marion,' and the other girl broke off what she was saying to stare at her suspiciously.

'Oh? I'm surprised you admit it, whatever it is.'

'Oh, yes.' Lesley forced herself to speak almost pleasantly, although she was trembling so much inside she could hardly speak coherently. Yet now that she had Marion's attention, she was loath to continue, as common sense reasserted itself in the face of her recklessness.

'Well?' Marion was getting impatient. 'What is it? Spit it out! Or don't you have the guts to admit you were lying?'

Her vindictiveness was the spur that drove Lesley on. Clasping her hands together, she said, 'You were right in saying my ability was to get pregnant, Marion.' And as the other girl's lips parted in silent protest, she added: 'I'm afraid after that night at the hotel, I've done it again.'

Whether or not she would have been able to sustain Marion's malevolent disbelief, she was never to know. As the damning words left her lips, there was a muffled oath from the door that led into the yard, and her horrified eyes turned to encounter Carne's incredulous gaze. She didn't know how long he had been there, but it was obvious he had heard her last statement, and she wished with all her heart that she could withdraw it.

'You're going to have a baby!' he said, through taut lips, and coward though she was, she could not deny it. Not then, not in front of Marion.

'You mean it's possible!' Now it was Marion herself who spoke and a look at Carne's face was answer enough. 'My God!' she exclaimed, and there was pain as well as bitterness in her voice. 'I thought you'd got over that stupid affair! But it seems I was wrong. How could you, Carne? How could you?'

Carne turned to look at her with grim eyes. 'I think you'd better go, Marion,' he said quietly. 'This has nothing to do with you.'

'It does. It does!' she cried desperately. 'You know how I feel about you . . .'

'And you know how I feel about you,' declared Carne flatly, and even through the tide of agony and humiliation that was washing over her, Lesley sensed the detachment in his words.

But what did it mean? What was he saying? That he had no feeling for Marion? It certainly sounded like it, and suddenly a wave of illumination swept doubt and suspicion aside. This was what Mary had meant when she said that Marion had married Aaron Bowland out of pique. The other girl had married the old man to try and make Carne jealous, knowing full well that Aaron had few more years to live. Shrewd and calculating it might have been, but it was the sort of thing Marion might have done.

Now Marion had turned towards the door, but she wasn't quite ready to concede defeat. 'You think you hold all the cards, don't you, Lesley?' she demanded maliciously. 'Well, don't forget there's still Carne's mother to contend with. She'll never accept you at Raventhorpe. She never has— and she never will!'

And as if to emphasise the fact, at that moment there came a heavy hammering on the floor above their heads.

'That's her now,' said Marion triumphantly, but as Carne moved towards the door, Lesley's hand on his arm stopped him.

'Let me,' she said, and leaving Marion and Carne together, she hurried unsteadily up the stairs.

Mrs Radley was sitting up in bed when she opened her door, and when she saw Lesley her mouth drew into a tight line.

'Oh, so it's you!' she said, the dying blemishes on her weather worn features giving her a mottled look. 'I might have known. What's going on? Where's Mary? I want my afternoon tea.'

'Mary?' Lesley's lips framed the name. 'But I—well, Mary's not here.'

'Not here? Not here?' Mrs Radley frowned. 'What do you mean? Where is she? She's always here.'

Lesley hesitated, and Carne's mother regarded her suspiciously. 'Well? What is it? Where is she? What's she doing? Oh, no—she's not got this blessed disease, too, has she?'

'No.' Lesley decided she had to be honest. 'She—she left.'

'Left?' Mrs Radley glared at her. 'Talk sense, girl. Why would Mary leave? She's been here—what? Fifteen years!'

'I know, but—well, apparently she and Marion——'

'Marion? Marion? What has she got to do with it?'

'I—I believe she and Mary had—had a difference of opinion.'

'Indeed?' Carne's mother plucked at the bedspread. 'What about? You?'

'No.' Lesley was indignant. 'I just got here a few hours ago. As a matter of fact, it was—to do with Jeremy.'

'Huh!' Mrs Radley didn't express any disbelief. 'Well, that doesn't surprise me. Not the maternal type, isn't Marion. Should have seen that before. Mind, I'm not saying that young rascal hasn't been a nuisance, because he has! Demanding attention at all times of the day and night, running his father and Marion, and Mary too, if she'd let him, off their feet. But when it comes down to it, Mary's got more compassion in her little finger than Marion's got in her whole body!'

Hiding her astonishment at this unexpected speech, Lesley managed to nod and say: 'Apparently Jeremy wet the bed and——'

'Ah!' Mrs Radley was nodding now, and Lesley took the opportunity to ask how she was feeling.

'Me?' The old woman sniffed. 'Better—now.' Her lips twisted wryly. 'I should have had more sense, but that boy of yours wanted a puppy, and I took him over to Minters to see their litter. I knew their boy had measles, but I never thought we'd get it. Kept out of the house on purpose, but there you are.'

'Yes.' Lesley had never had such a civil conversation with her mother-in-law. But she was not foolish enough to imagine anything had changed between them because of it. Nevertheless, it was reassuring to know that Carne's mother could behave civilly towards her.

As if to underline this fact, Mrs Radley chose that moment to return to the attack. 'What are you doing here anyway? Who told you I was ill? Not Marion, I'll be bound.'

'No. It was Mary,' answered Lesley honestly, wondering what was going on downstairs, wondering what else Marion was saying. 'She rang the flat and spoke to my mother. When I heard—I came.'

'Hmm.' A little of the old antagonism sparked in Carne's mother's eyes. 'Well, you're a bit late, as it happens. The worst's over. We're both on the mend. And Marion's been a great help.' Then she paused, catching her lower lip between her teeth. 'But Mary walking out . . .' She shook her head. 'That's not like Mary.' She shook her head. 'Marion will have to see her, speak to her, ask her to come back. We can't do without Mary.'

Lesley moved her shoulders in a helpless gesture, and as she did so, she heard someone coming up the stairs. It could only be Carne and she said quickly: 'I don't know whether Mary would listen to Marion. They—well, they don't like one another very much.'

'Perhaps not.' Mrs Radley conceded the point unwillingly. 'But people's likes and dislikes can't always be considered. Mary's needed here. Who's going to do the cooking and cleaning, the washing and the ironing, if Mary's not here?'

'Perhaps Lesley will help us out herself,' declared her husband's voice behind her, and she turned to stare anxiously into his vaguely strained features. 'This is her home, after all. Her husband and child are here. Perhaps now she'll decide that this is where she belongs.'

CHAPTER TEN

How Lesley got out of that room, she could never afterwards remember. All she knew was that she muttered something about hearing Jeremy calling her, but after closing Carne's mother's door, she hastened quickly down the stairs.

The kitchen was empty. Apparently Marion had gone, and she cringed from the recollection of what had been said. How could she have been so stupid? How could she have allowed Marion to goad her into saying something so outrageous? And how could she tell Carne that it had been a lie?

Why had she said it? Perhaps she should ask herself that question first. After all, for someone who professed such little interest in her husband, she behaved in a totally unreasonable way. Why should it matter to her that Marion was making herself at home at Raventhorpe? Why should she care if Carne turned to her now? Years ago, things had been different. She had loved Carne then, loved him desperately, cared that her marriage was splintering before her eyes. But all that should be over now. Surely that was why she had left, so why should it surprise her or still have the power to hurt her?

She moved to the sink and pressed her clenched fists against the cool steel of the drainer. The unpalatable truth was that in spite of everything that had gone before, she still cared about her marriage, still cared about Carne; and her jealousy over Jeremy had merely been a blind to hide

her own feelings. Of course she hadn't wanted Jeremy to
come to Raventhorpe. But not because she cared about his
clothes or the things Carne and his mother might say to him.
She was afraid of herself, of her own feelings, of the kindling torment associating with Carne again after all this time
might arouse. Marion had been right about one thing—her
independence was only a shield, to protect her own vulner-
ability.

She had not been aware of anyone's approach, and when
hard fingers stroked the length of her arm from elbow to
wrist she started violently.

'Lesley!' Carne's voice was low and passionate, close behind her ear. 'Lesley, I should have been the first to know
—not Marion Bowland.'

Lesley glanced round at him tautly, unable to meet the
reproachful darkness of his eyes. What was he thinking?
she wondered desperately. Had her announcement taken
him off guard? Or had it swung a kind of mental balance in
her favour? Had supposing he was to be a father again
temporarily banished the contempt he felt for her, or was
he simply feeling sorry for her? Whatever, he would have
to be told the truth . . .

'Carne . . .' she began, but he shook his head, breaking in
on her, bracing himself with his hands against the drainer
unit.

'You don't have to make excuses,' he said, and his voice
had harshened a little. 'I know I'm to blame.'

'Carne, you don't understand——'

'Nor do you,' he countered, not letting her finish. 'God
knows, it's what I hoped would happen!'

'Wh-what you hoped?' Lesley stared at his profile. 'I
don't know what you mean.'

'I know. I know.' A smile of self-derision twisted his expression. 'Do you think I don't know how you're feeling

right now?' He shook his head again. 'Lesley, let me tell you the truth——'

'Carne, I——'

'No, listen to me. Please!' He looked at her, and the pain in his eyes brought a choking lump to her throat that successfully robbed her of speech. 'When you walked out on me, I never intended it to go so far.' He paused. 'Believe it or not, but I really believed that all you needed was time. Time to reorientate yourself, time to get things into perspective, time to realise that you loved me and would come back to me.' He moved his shoulders helplessly. 'Even stopping seeing Jeremy was a calculated risk I had to take. I knew that so long as I kept appearing in your life, you would never feel really free of me. So I kept away.'

'But, Carne——'

'Let me finish . . .' He bent his head, his knuckles white through the brown skin of his hands. 'So—I guess it would be about a year after I'd last seen you, I decided it had gone on long enough. I told my mother that I was going to London to ask you to come back.' He sighed. 'That was about six weeks before her accident. After that . . .' He spread his hands. 'Things were never the same again.'

'You should have written——'

'I did write. To your mother.' He expelled his breath noisily. 'She kept me informed, as you've already accused. Then, when I heard you were sending Jeremy to boarding school, I decided that maybe I was a fool imagining you would ever come back. You had your own life to lead, and not even Jeremy was going to get in your way——'

'That's not true! My mother couldn't be expected——'

'Oh, I know. I *know* there were reasons. But you didn't— not then. That was when I decided I would have my son if nothing else.'

'Carne!'

He turned his head to give her a bitter look. 'Yes. Foolish, wasn't it? I even fooled myself that when I saw you again, I'd feel nothing but contempt. But it didn't happen—and you know it! From the minute you came into your mother's living room, I knew I'd made a terrible mistake, but it was too late then to draw back. And so I decided to fight, can you believe that? To fight, in the only way I knew how.'

Lesley couldn't meet his gaze. Her own heart was pounding so heavily, she could hardly think, but what was coming over loud and clear was that Carne was telling her he had never stopped wanting her.

Putting some space between them, she burst out: 'Why did you let me leave Raventhorpe?'

'Why did *I* let you leave? Could I have stopped you?'

'Of course.' She flicked a glance at him. 'If you feel like this now, why didn't you feel like it then? Why did you let me think you were involved with Marion Harvey? Or were you? And has that worn off now?'

His eyes darkened angrily, and his hands reached for her, jerking her roughly towards him. 'Don't ever say that to me again!' he commanded savagely. 'You *know* there was nothing—nothing like *that* between Marion and me.'

'Do I?'

'You should.' His eyes moved hungrily over her face. 'I did everything I could to show you I only cared about you.'

'Did you?' She stared at him. 'Like—like moving out of our bedroom?'

'Yes.' His fingers dug into her flesh. 'Damn you, yes.' He moved his head in a frustrated gesture. 'It wasn't *our* bedroom any more, was it? It was yours—and the baby's. Once Jeremy was born, you were only interested in him, not in anything else.'

'You can't believe that!'

'Can't I?' Carne's lips tightened. 'Believe me, a man can believe anything if he convinces himself it's true. Didn't you convince yourself that I was involved with Marion? Just to justify the real reasons you had for leaving?'

Lesley swallowed. 'Which were?'

'Independence—ambition. You name it. Being a farmer's wife had become a bore. The novelty had worn off. You needed something to blame, so you blamed my relationship with Marion.'

Lesley blinked. Was it true? Had they both been so blind? Had Mrs Radley and Marion only underlined the basic insecurities of their relationship? If it were true . . . If it were true . . .

Now Carne was drawing her closer, his hands sliding possessively over her hips, his eyes narrowed to a sensual awareness. She could feel the heaving throbbing of his heart against her breast, and sensed the urgent message of his body.

Yet her own duplicity weighed heavily inside her. It was incredible to believe that Carne had not stopped loving her, but how much of this confession would she have heard if he had not thought she was pregnant again? Was this only to reassure her? Could he be lying? And how was she ever to know?

'Lesley . . .' He said her name against her ear, his breath warm and disturbing in that small orifice. 'Lesley, I'm sorry if you resent the way I've behaved, I'm sorry if you don't want another baby, but there seemed no other way to get you back.'

Her reply was silenced by the pressure of his mouth. His parted lips took possession of hers, his tongue stroking their sensitive outline, awakening the ready response inside her. She had no will to resist the intoxicating hardness of his body that knew hers in so many different ways, no will to prevent the arched yielding to his masculinity that invited possession of an entirely different kind. How could she have lived so long without the demanding passion of his kiss, she wondered dazedly, without the sweet sensuality of his love?

With a little cry, she wound her arms around his neck, pushing her fingers through the smooth thickness of his hair, uncaring for the moment as she pressed herself against him that there were still things to explain between them, uncaring of anything but the pulsating power of the emotion that gripped them.

'Lesley,' he said at last, hoarsely. 'Lesley, don't make me lose all control or I'll take you here—now—just as we are!' His eyes were dark and tormented. 'There are still things that need to be said.'

'I know.' His words were sobering and she drew back sufficiently to run a smoothing hand over her own tumbled hair, to examine the unbuttoned provocation of her shirt. 'Carne, I have something to tell you, too. I didn't come here because—because I was pregnant. Mary—Mary teleph——'

His hands tightened on the smooth skin at her waist, his eyes still glazed with emotion. 'Did Mary tell you that I asked her to ring?' he asked thickly. 'Did she tell you that?'

'No!' For a moment Lesley was too confused to continue. '*You* asked Mary to ring?'

'Yes.' He bent his head to touch her throat with his lips, and their heat sent a wave of colour sweeping over her skin. 'You don't really think Mary has left, do you? After all these years?' He shook his head. 'No, we planned it between us. You had asked her to ring if Jeremy wasn't happy. For unhappy read unwell, and there you have it.'

'But she didn't ring until two days ago!' Lesley protested

and he brushed her cheek with his tongue.

'We didn't want to upset you. Jeremy was pretty sick to begin with, but once he began to get better . . .'

'But why didn't you just ask me to come back?'

'Would you have come?' His eyes narrowed disbelievingly. 'I asked you to stay, remember? But you turned me down.'

'That—that was for a dinner party . . .'

'You think my needing you would have been a sufficient inducement?' He shook his head again. 'I needed you—I *always* needed you—but I had always believed you wanted your freedom. I had Mary telephone you because I hoped once you heard the boy was sick that you would come, for his sake if for no other. Time was slipping away. I knew if the holidays were over and Jeremy returned to London, I might never have another chance. I could never have asked you to stay . . .'

'But you're asking me now,' she breathed huskily, and his lips probed the pointed fullness of her breast.

'Yes,' he agreed honestly, but there was unspoken uncertainty in his eyes as he lifted his head. 'But only because . . .' He broke off. 'Is it selfish of me, Lesley? Am I too possessive? Is it too much to hope that given a second chance, you might learn to enjoy living here? Or will what I've done always stand between us?'

Lesley couldn't take any more. With a muffled exclamation she fled out of the house and across the stableyard, not stopping until she reached the Mini, sitting in a pool of mud. The rain had washed manure across the yard, and she slipped and slid as she sought to climb behind the wheel. That she succeeded at all was due more to rugged determination than expertise, and turning the ignition, she fired the engine and reversed away.

The car lurched a little, and then steadied beneath her

hands as she drove blindly down the track towards the road. The persistent rain lashed at the windscreen, but she was not cold. On the contrary, she was sweating, but it was as much with apprehension as anything. What Carne must be thinking if her, what interpretation he might put on her behaviour she could only guess, and her head ached from the strain of trying to escape the inevitable torment of her thoughts. All her life, she had been running away from one thing or another, she thought bitterly, and Carne would never forgive her for making a fool of him all over again.

She was still some distance from the cattle grid when the Landrover suddenly crashed through the hedge in front of her, causing her to swerve violently and jam on her brakes. For a moment, she couldn't understand what was happening, but then Carne swung down from the four-wheeled vehicle and she knew her running days were over. At least, for the time being. He strode across to the Mini and wrenched open the door, hauling her out with all the care and consideration of a gorilla, and when she tried to recover her breath, he put his face close to hers and said:

'For God's sake, Lesley! Are you trying to kill yourself?'

'I—I thought you were trying to—to do that!' she stammered, unable to summon any words of anger or explanation, and with a savage oath he flung her towards the Land-rover.

'Get in!' he said. 'We're going somewhere where we can talk, without interruption.'

The rugged journey across the fields to Bowland's Dam was accomplished in absolute silence, Lesley desperately trying to voice the words of explanation which would not come. Crazy thoughts went round her head, thoughts like letting him go on believing she was pregnant and hoping it would become a reality, thoughts like telling him she had never cared about her career except when she needed a bolt-hole to crawl into.

The dam had, as Carne had told her weeks before, been built up to form a quasi-natural pool, fed from moorland springs, whose water was icy cold. In spite of the rain, Lesley jumped down from the Landrover as soon as Carne stopped the engine, and walked quickly to the edge of the pool, looking down mutely into its lucid depths.

'Now . . .' Carne had come up behind her, and as the rain wet his shirt, it moulded the muscles of his shoulders more closely. 'If this is private enough for you, tell me why you rushed out of the house like a mad thing when I asked you to stay? Was I wrong? Does being pregnant mean nothing to you? Do you still want your freedom?'

Lesley wrapped her arms about herself, and refused to look at him. 'No. Yes. And no,' she said tensely, and sensed his silent imprecation.

'Lesley——'

'All right.' She swung round to face him, the rain pouring down her face, mingling with the tears that came so readily from her eyes. She was conscious of the bedraggled picture she must present, and thought how fitting it was that she should be the one to suffer in this way. 'All right,' she said again, holding up her head. 'The truth is—I'm not pregnant. Do you hear me? I'm not going to have a baby.'

Carne's face was as cold and still as if it was carved from stone. 'You're not?'

'No, I'm not.'

'But——' His brows drew together. 'You told Marion——'

'Oh, yes, yes, I told Marion I was. What else was I supposed to do? Let her go on telling me how useless I was? How inefficient? How inadequate? Having her tell me that you didn't care about me, that you never cared about me? Disbelieving me when I told her we'd spent a night together! Well, she believes me now. *You* convinced her of that!'

A little of the chill had left his face as he listened to this tirade. 'What are you saying? Why should it matter to you what Marion believes?'

'Oh, you know! You know!' she cried imploringly. 'I love you! I've always loved you. Only, like you, I was too proud to beg!'

'*Lesley . . .*'

The throbbing timbre of his voice drove her into his arms, uncaring that they were wet, uncaring of the rain, uncaring of anything but their mutual need of one another.

'God, I was afraid,' he muttered, burying his face in the warm hollow of her throat. 'I knew you could get a divorce any time you wanted, and I was sure that was what you wanted.'

Lesley's laugh was half sob. 'Then we've both been fools, haven't we?' she breathed. 'I—are you very disappointed—about the baby?'

'Disappointed? Now?' He shook his head, cupping her face with his hands. 'Does this mean you're staying? Despite everything?'

'Try and drive me away!'

'I wouldn't do that,' he muttered. 'And I'll take damn good care no one else does either.'

'Your mother,' she breathed. 'What will she say?'

'A lot, I expect,' he admitted wryly. 'But we've been fighting over you for years. She might just decide to give in.'

'I doubt it.' Lesley was philosophical. 'But Jeremy will be delighted. I have the feeling I'd have split him down the middle if I'd tried to take him away from here.'

'What about school?' Carne quirked an eyebrow at her and Lesley smiled.

'Leaving Taunton won't worry Jeremy. He wasn't happy there.'

'I know. He told me. He also told me why I'd been elevated to the role of pilot.'

Lesley stroked his lips with her fingers. 'Where did you go to school?'

'The local grammar,' he told her, half apologetically, and she laughed.

'Then I'm sure Jeremy will be happy there, too.' She frowned. 'You haven't told me why Mary pretended to leave.'

'Oh, that.' Carne grinned. 'I hoped that finding Marion here would tip the balance, one way or the other. It was a calculated risk.'

Lesley absorbed this, and then she said: 'Mary said there were rows between you and your mother after—after I walked out. Before your mother had her accident.'

'Before and after,' said Carne dryly. 'Although for a time my hands were tied. She was quite ill for a while.'

'Mary also said that—that Marion married Aaron Bowland out of—of pique. Why did she say that?'

Carne's lean features darkened with colour. 'Mary seems to have said an awful lot in a short time, doesn't she?' He sighed. 'Well, it may be true, but I doubt it. It is true that after you left, she began to make quite a nuisance of herself. I had to—well, tell her how it was.'

'And how was it?' breathed Lesley, putting her hands on his forearms, and reaching up to his mouth.

'How it's always been,' he muttered, and then with a groan, he drew her down on to the rain-sodden turf and covered her body with his own. 'This is madness, do you know that?' he demanded, as the prickling blades of grass stroked her bare midriff with sensuous softness. 'We'll very likely catch pneumonia!'

'Lance said if I didn't get back by Wednesday, I was out of a job anyway,' she whispered softly. 'I won't be back by Wednesday, will I, darling . . .?'

Harlequin

COLLECTION
EDITIONS OF 1978

Harlequin's Collection 12
ANDREA BLAKE
Night of the Hurrica

Harlequin's Collection 106   1.25
ANNE WEALE
If This Is Love

**50 great stories
of special beauty
and significance**

$1.25
each novel

In 1976 we introduced the first 100 Harlequin Collections—a selection of titles chosen from our best sellers of the past 20 years. This series, a trip down memory lane, proved how great romantic fiction can be timeless and appealing from generation to generation. The theme of love and romance is eternal, and, when placed in the hands of talented, creative, authors whose true gift lies in their ability to write from the heart, the stories reach a special level of brilliance that the passage of time cannot dim. Like a treasured heirloom, an antique of superb craftsmanship, a beautiful gift from someone loved—these stories too, have a special significance that transcends the ordinary. **$1.25 each novel**

Here are your 1978
Harlequin Collection Editions...

Original Harlequin Romance numbers in brackets

ORDER FORM
Harlequin Reader Service

In U.S.A.
MPO Box 707
Niagara Falls, N.Y. 14302

In Canada
649 Ontario St.,
Stratford, Ontario, N5A 6W2

Please send me the following Harlequin Collection novels. I am enclosing my check or money order for $1.25 for each novel ordered, plus 25¢ to cover postage and handling.

☐ 102	☐ 115	☐ 128	☐ 140
☐ 103	☐ 116	☐ 129	☐ 141
☐ 104	☐ 117	☐ 130	☐ 142
☐ 105	☐ 118	☐ 131	☐ 143
☐ 106	☐ 119	☐ 132	☐ 144
☐ 107	☐ 120	☐ 133	☐ 145
☐ 108	☐ 121	☐ 134	☐ 146
☐ 109	☐ 122	☐ 135	☐ 147
☐ 110	☐ 123	☐ 136	☐ 148
☐ 111	☐ 124	☐ 137	☐ 149
☐ 112	☐ 125	☐ 138	☐ 150
☐ 113	☐ 126	☐ 139	☐ 151
☐ 114	☐ 127		

Number of novels checked @
$1.25 each = $ _____
N.Y. and N.J. residents add
appropriate sales tax $ _____

Postage and handling $ ___.25___

TOTAL $ _____

NAME _____
(Please Print)
ADDRESS _____

CITY _____

STATE/PROV. _____

ZIP/POSTAL CODE _____

PRS 262

A

Offer expires December 31, 1978